# PUSH

# PUSH

a novel by **SAPPHIRE**

Alfred A.
Knopf

New York

1996

F

THIS IS A BORZOI BOOK
PUBLISHED BY ALFRED A. KNOPF, INC.

http://www.randomhouse.com/

Grateful acknowledgment is made to Alfred A. Knopf, Inc.,
for permission to reprint "Mother to Son" from *Selected
Poems* by Langston Hughes, copyright © 1926 by Alfred A.
Knopf, Inc., copyright renewed 1954 by Langston Hughes.

Library of Congress Cataloging-in-Publication Data
Sapphire, [date]
Push / Sapphire. — 1st ed.
p.    cm.
ISBN 0-679-44626-5
I. Title.
PS3569.A63P87   1996
813'.54—dc20            96-16516
                        CIP

Manufactured in the United States of America

First Edition

*For children everywhere.
And for my teachers Eavan Boland,
James D. Merritt,
and most especially
Susan Fromberg Schaeffer.*

ACKNOWLEDGMENTS

I wish to thank and acknowledge Susan Fromberg Schaeffer, Victoria Wilson, Charlotte Sheedy, Neeti Madan, Catherine McKinley, Jacqueline Woodson, Ellen Ray, Sheilah Mabry, Eve Ensler, and Kimberly Goodman.

I also wish to thank and acknowledge the Millay Colony and The Writers Room.

*If thou be one whose heart the holy forms*
*Of young imagination have kept pure,*
*Stranger! henceforth be warned; and know, that pride,*
*Howe'er disguised in its own majesty,*
*Is littleness; that he who feels contempt*
*For any living thing, hath faculties*
*Which he has never used; that thought with him*
*Is in its infancy. The man, whose eye*
*is ever on himself, doth look on one,*
*The least of nature's works, one who might move*
*The wise man to that scorn which wisdom holds*
*Unlawful, ever. O, be wiser thou!*
*Instructed that true knowledge leads to love . . .*

WILLIAM WORDSWORTH


*Every blade of grass has its Angel that bends over it*
*and whispers, "Grow, grow."*

THE TALMUD

PUSH

I was left back when I was twelve because I had a baby for my fahver. That was in 1983. I was out of school for a year. This gonna be my second baby. My daughter got Down Sinder. She's retarded. I had got left back in the second grade too, when I was seven, 'cause I couldn't read (and I still peed on myself). I should be in the eleventh grade, getting ready to go into the twelf' grade so I can gone 'n graduate. But I'm not. I'm in the ninfe grade.

I got suspended from school 'cause I'm pregnant which I don't think is fair. I ain' did nothin'!

My name is Claireece Precious Jones. I don't know why I'm telling you that. Guess 'cause I don't know how far I'm gonna go with this story, or whether it's even a story or why I'm talkin'; whether I'm gonna start from the beginning or right from here or two weeks from now. Two weeks from now? Sure you can do anything when you talking or writing, it's not like living when you can only do what you doing. Some people tell a story 'n it don't make no sense or be true. But I'm gonna try to make sense and tell the truth, else what's the fucking use? Ain' enough lies and shit out there already?

So, OK, it's Thursday, September twenty-four 1987 and I'm walking down the hall. I look good, smell good—fresh, clean. It's hot but I do not take off my leather jacket even though it's hot, it might get stolen or lost. Indian summer, Mr Wicher say. I don't know why he call it that. What he mean is, it's *hot*, 90 degrees, like summer days. And there is no, none, I mean *none*, air conditioning in this mutherfucking building. The building I'm talking about is, of course, I.S. 146 on 134th Street between Lenox Avenue and Adam Clayton Powell Jr Blvd. I am walking down the hall from home-room to first period maff. Why they put some shit like maff first period I do not know. Maybe to gone 'n git it over with. I actually don't mind maff as much as I had thought I would. I jus' fall in Mr Wicher's class sit down. We don't have assigned seats in Mr Wicher's class, we can sit anywhere we want. I sit in the same seat everyday, in the back, last row, next to the door. Even though I know that back door be locked. I don't say nuffin' to him. He don't say nuffin' to me, *now*. First day he say, "Class turn the book pages to page 122 please." I don't move. He say, "Miss Jones, I *said* turn the book pages to page 122." I say, "Mutherfucker I ain't deaf!" The whole class laugh. He turn red. He slam his han' down on the book and say, "Try to have some disci-pline." He a skinny little white man about five feets four inches. A peckerwood as my mother would say. I look at him 'n say, "I can slam too. You wanna slam?" 'N I pick up my book 'n slam it down on the desk hard. The class laugh some more. He say, "Miss Jones I would appreciate it if you would leave the room right NOW." I say, "I ain' going nowhere mutherfucker till the bell ring. I came here to learn maff and you gon' teach me." He look like a bitch just got a train pult on her. He don't know what to do. He try to recoup, be cool, say, "Well, if you want to learn, calm down—" "I'm calm," I tell him. He say, "If you want to learn, shut up and open your book." His face is red, he is shaking. I back off. I have won. I guess.

I didn't want to hurt him or embarrass him like that you know. But I couldn't let him, anybody, know, page 122 look like page 152, 22, 3, 6, 5—all the pages look alike to me. 'N I really do want to learn. Everyday I tell myself something gonna happen, some shit like on TV. I'm gonna break through or somebody gonna break through to me—I'm gonna learn, catch up, be normal, change my seat to the front of the class. But again, it has not been that day.

But thas the first day I'm telling you about. Today is not the first day and like I said I was on my way to maff class when Mrs Lichenstein snatch me out the hall to her office. I'm really mad 'cause actually I like maff even though I don't do nuffin', don't open my book even. I jus' sit there for fifty minutes. I don't cause trouble. In fac' some of the other natives get restless I break on 'em. I say, "Shut up mutherfuckers I'm tryin' to learn something." First they laugh like trying to pull me into fuckin' with Mr Wicher and disrupting the class. Then I get up 'n say, "Shut up mutherfuckers I'm tryin' to learn something." The coons clowning look confuse, Mr Wicher look confuse. But I'm big, five feet nine-ten, I weigh over two hundred pounds. Kids is scared of me. "Coon fool," I tell one kid done jumped up. "Sit down, stop ackin' silly." Mr Wicher look at me confuse but grateful. I'm like the polices for Mr Wicher. I keep law and order. I like him, I pretend he is my husband and we live together in Weschesser, wherever that is.

I can see by his eyes Mr Wicher like me too. I wish I could tell him about all the pages being the same but I can't. I'm getting pretty good grades. I usually do. I just wanna gone get the fuck out of I.S. 146 and go to high school and get my diploma.

Anyway I'm in Mrs Lichenstein's office. She's looking at me, I'm looking at her. I don't say nuffin'. Finally she say, "So Claireece, I see we're expecting a little visitor." But it's not like a question, she's telling me. I still don't say nuffin'. She staring at me, from behind her big wooden desk, she got her white bitch hands folded together on top her desk.

"Claireece."

Everybody call me Precious. I got three names—Claireece Precious Jones. Only mutherfuckers I hate call me Claireece.

"How old are you Claireece?"

White cunt box got my file on her desk. I see it. I ain't that late to lunch. Bitch know how old I am.

"Sixteen is ahh rather ahh"—she clear her throat—"*old* to still be in junior high school."

I still don't say nuffin'. She know so much let her ass do the talking.

"Come now, you are pregnant, aren't you Claireece?"

She asking now, a few seconds ago the hoe just *knew* what I was.

"Claireece?"

She tryin' to talk all gentle now and shit.

"Claireece, I'm talking to you."

I still don't say nuffin'. This hoe is keeping me from maff class. I like maff class. Mr Wicher like me in there, need me to keep those rowdy niggers in line. He nice, wear a dope suit *every* day. He do not come to school looking like some of these other nasty ass teachers.

"I don't want to miss no more of maff class," I tell stupid ass Mrs Lichenstein.

She look at me like I said I wanna suck a dog's dick or some shit. What's with this cunt bucket? (That's what my muver call women she don't like, cunt buckets. I kinda get it and I kinda don't get it, but I like the way it sounds so I say it too.)

I get up to go, Mrs Lichenstein ax me to please sit down, she not through with me yet. But I'm through with her, thas what she don't get.

"This is your *second* baby?" she says. I wonder what else it say in that file with my name on it. I hate her.

"I think we should have a parent-teacher conference Claireece—me, you, and your mom."

"For what?" I say. "I ain' done nuffin'. I doose my work. I ain' in no trouble. My grades is good."

Mrs Lichenstein look at me like I got three arms or a bad odor out my pussy or something.

What my muver gon' do I want to say. What is she gonna do? But I don't say that. I jus' say, "My muver is busy."

"Well maybe I could arrange to come to your house—" The look on my face musta hit her, which is what I was gonna do if she said one more word. Come to my house! Nosy ass white bitch! I don't think so! We don't be coming to your house in Weschesser or wherever the fuck you freaks live. Well I be damned, I done heard everything, white bitch wanna visit.

"Well then Claireece, I'm afraid I'm going to have to suspend you—"

"For what!"

"You're pregnant and—"

"You can't suspend me for being pregnant, I got rights!"

"Your attitude Claireece is one of total uncooperation—"

I reached over the desk. I was gonna yank her fat ass out that chair. She fell backwards trying to get away from me 'n started screaming, "SECURITY SECURITY!"

I was out the door and on the street and I could still hear her stupid ass screaming, "SECURITY SECURITY!"


"Precious!" That's my mother calling me.

I don't say nothin'. She been staring at my stomach. I know what's coming. I keep washing dishes. We had fried chicken, mashed potatoes, gravy, green beans, and Wonder bread for dinner. I don't know how many months pregnant I am. I don't wanna stand here 'n hear Mama call me slut. Holler 'n shout on me all day like she did the last time. Slut! Nasty ass tramp! What you been doin'! Who! Who! WHOoooo like owl in Walt Disney movie I seen one time. Whooo? Ya wanna know who—

"Claireece Precious Jones I'm talkin' to you!"

I still don't answer her. I was standing at this sink the last time I was pregnant when them pains hit, *wump!* Ahh wump! I never felt no shit like that before. Sweat was breaking out on my forehead, pain like fire was eating me up. I jus' standing there 'n pain hit me, then pain go sit down, then pain git up 'n hit me harder! 'N she standing there *screaming* at me, "Slut! Goddam slut! You fuckin' cow! I don't believe this, right under my nose. You been high tailing it round here." Pain hit me again, then *she* hit me. I'm on the floor groaning, "Mommy please, Mommy please, please Mommy! Mommy! Mommy! MOMMY!" Then she KICK me side of my face! "Whore! Whore!" she screamin'. Then Miz West live down the hall pounding on the door, hollering "Mary! Mary! What you doin'! You gonna kill that chile! She need help not no beating, is you crazy!"

Mama say, "She shoulda tole me she was pregnant!"

"Jezus Mary, you didn't know. *I* knew, the whole building knew. Are you crazy—"

"Don't tell me nothin' about my own chile—"

"Nine-one-one! Nine-one-one! Nine-one-one!" Miz West screamin' now. She call Mama a fool.

Pain walking on me now. Jus' stomping on me. I can't see hear, I jus' screamin', "Mommy! Mommy!"

Some mens, these ambulance mens, I don't see 'em or hear 'em come in. But I look up from the pain and he dere. This Spanish guy in EMS uniform. He push me back on a cushion. I'm like in a ball from the pain. He say, "RELAX!" The pain stabbing me wif a knife and this spic talking 'bout relax.

He touch my forehead put his other hand on the side of my belly. "What's your name?" he say. "Huh?" I say. "Your name?" "Precious," I say. He say, "Precious, it's almost here. I want you to push, you hear me momi, when that shit hit you again, go with it and push, Preshecita. *Push.*"

And I did.

And always after that I look for someone with his face and eyes in Spanish people. He coffee-cream color, good hair. I remember that. God. I think he was god.

No man was never nice like that to me before. I ask at the hospital behind him, "Where that guy help me?" They say, "Hush girl you jus' had a baby."

But I can't hush 'cause they keep asking me questions. My name? Precious Jones. Claireece Precious Jones to be exact. Birth date? November 4, 1970. Where? *"Here,"* I say, "right chere in Harlem Hospital." *"Nineteen seventy?"* the nurse say confuse quiet. Then she say, "How old are you?" I say, "Twelve." I was heavy at twelve too, nobody get I'm twelve 'less I tell them. I'm tall. I jus' know I'm over two hundred 'cause the needle on the scale in the bathroom stop there it don't can go no further. Last time they want to weigh me at school I say no. Why for, I know I'm fat. So what. Next topic for the day.

But this not school nurse now, this Harlem Hospital where I was borned, where me and my baby got tooked after it was borned on the kitchen floor at 444 Lenox Avenue. This nurse slim butter-color woman. She lighter than some Spanish womens but I know she black. I can tell. It's something about being a nigger ain't color. This nurse same as me. A lot of black people with nurse cap or big car or light skin same as me but don't know it. I'm so tired I jus' want to disappear. I wish Miss Butter would leave me alone but she jus' staring at me, her eyes getting bigger and bigger. She say she need to get some more information for the birth certificate.

It still tripping me out that I had a baby. I mean I knew I was pregnant, knew how I got pregnant. I been knowing a man put his dick in you, gush white stuff in your booty you could get pregnant. I'm twelve now, I been knowing about that since I was five or six, maybe I always known about pussy and dick. I can't remember not knowing. No, I can't remember a time I did not know. But thas all I knowed. I didn't know how long it take, what's happening inside, nothing, I didn't know nothing.

The nurse is saying something I don't hear. I hear kids at school. Boy say I'm laffing ugly. He say, "Claireece is so ugly she laffing ugly." His fren' say, "No, that fat bitch is crying ugly." Laff laff. Why I'm thinking about those stupid boys now I don't know.

"Mother," she say. "What's your mother's name?" I say, "Mary L Johnston" (L for Lee but my mother don't like Lee, soun' too country). "Where your mother born," she say. I say, "Greenwood, Mississippi." Nurse say, "You ever been there?" I say, "Naw, I never been nowhere." She say, "Reason I ask is I'm from Greenwood, Mississippi, myself." I say, "Oh," 'cause I know I'm spozed to say something.

"Father," she say. "What's your daddy's name?"

"Carl Kenwood Jones, born in the Bronx."

She say, "What's the baby's father's name?"

I say, "Carl Kenwood Jones, born in the same Bronx."

She quiet quiet. Say, "Shame, thas a shame. Twelve years old, twelve years old," she say over 'n over like she crazy (or in some shock or something). She look at me, butter skin, light eyes—I know boyz love her. She say, "Was you ever, I mean did you ever get to be a chile?" Thas a stupid question, did I ever get to be a chile? I *am* a chile.

I'm confuse, tired. I tell her I want to sleep. She put the bed down, I do go to sleep.

Somebody else there when I wake up. It's like the police or something. Wanna ax me some questions. I axes, "Where's my baby? I know I had one. I know that." New somebody in nurse cap sweet-smile me and say, "Yes, you did Miss Jones, you surely did." She moves the men in uniform suits back from my bed. Say my baby is in special intense care and I will get to see her soon and won't I please answer the nice men's questions. But they ain' nice men. They pigs. I ain' crazy. I don't tell them nothing.

All this from 1983 going through my head and my muver hollering at me, "Precious! Precious!" But my head not here, it in four years ago—first baby. I was standing at this sink when the pain hit me, and she hit me.

My hand slip down in the dishwater, grab the butcher knife. She bedda not hit me, I ain' lyin'! If she hit me I will stab her ass to def, you hear me!

"Precious! You done lost your mind? Just standing up there staring into spaces. I'm talkin' to you!"

Like thas something.

"I was thinkin'," I say.

"You thinkin' while I'm talkin' to you?"

She say this like I'm burnin' hunnert dollar bills.

The buzzer ring. I wonder who it could be. Don't nobody ring our bell 'less it's crack addicts trying to get in the building. I hate crack addicts. They give the race a bad name.

"Go tell them assholes to stop ringing the bell," she say. She closer to the door than me but I mean my muver don't move 'less she has to. I mean that. When I go to answer the buzzer I realize I'm still grabbing the knife. I hate my muver sometimes. She is ugly I think sometime.

I press TALK on the intercom and holler, "Stop ringing the goddam buzzer mutherfucker!" and go back to the kitchen to finish the dishes.

The buzzer ring again. I go back. "Stop ringing the goddam buzzer," I say again. The mutherfucker ring again. "Stop it!" It ring *again*. "STOP IT!" I shout again. It ring again. My muver jump in and say, "Press LISTEN stupid!" I wanna say I ain' stupid but I know I am so I don't say nothin', 'cause also I don't want her to go hit me, 'cause I know from my hand in the dishwater holding the butcher knife, I am through being hit. I am going to stab her she ever hit Precious Jones again. I press LISTEN. "It's Sondra Lichenstein for Claireece Jones and Ms Mary Johnston." *Mrs Lichenstein!* What that hoe want? She want me to hit her for real this time.

"Who that Precious?" my muver say. I say, "White bitch from school." "What she want?" my muver say. "I don't know." "Ask her," my muver say. I press TALK 'n say, "What you want?" Then I press LISTEN and Mrs Lichenstein say, "I want to talk to you about your education." This bitch crazy. I was going to school everyday till her honky ass snatch me out the hall, fuck with my mind, make me go off on her, suspend me from school jus' because I'm pregnant—you know, *end up* my education. Now her white ass out on Lenox Avenue talkin' 'bout she wanna talk to me about my education. Lord where is crack addicts when you need 'em. "What all this about Precious?" my muver asks. My muver don't want no white shit like Mrs Lichenstein social worker teacher ass nosing around here. My muver don't want to get cut off, welfare that is. And that's what white shit like Mrs Lichenstein comin' to visit result in. If I wasn't pregnant and having trouble with the stairs, I run down and kick her ass. My muver say, "Eighty-six that bitch." I says into the intercom, "Hasta la vista, baby." That's Spanish for good-bye but when niggers say it, it's like, kiss my ass. Ring go buzzer again. I don't believe this retarded hoe. I press TALK 'n say, "Git outta here Mrs Lichenstein 'fore I kick your ass." The bell go ring. I press LISTEN. "Claireece I am so sorry about Thursday. I had only wanted to help you. I . . . Mr Wicher says you're one of his best students, that you have an aptitude for math." She pause like she thinking what to say next, then she say, "I've called a Ms McKnight at Higher Education Alternative/Each One Teach One. It's an alternative school." She pause again, say, "Claireece, are you listening?" I press TALK. "Yeah," I say. "OK, as I was saying I've called Ms McKnight at Each One Teach One. It's located on the nineteenth floor of the Hotel Theresa on 125th Street. That's not too far from here." I press TALK. "I know where the Hotel Theresa is," I say to her, Bitch, I say to myself. I press LISTEN again, these crackers think you don't know nothin'. She say, "The phone number is 555-0831. I told them about you." Mrs Lichenstein stop. "Call or just drop in, the nineteenth floor—" I press TALK tell her I heard her the first time. My heart is all warm—half of it at least—thinking about Mr Wicher say I'm a good student. The other half could jus' jump out my chest and kick Mrs Lichenstein's ass. No more rings—so I guess that mean she got the message.

I go to sleep thinking nineteenth floor Hotel Theresa, an alternative. I don't know what an alternative is but I feel I want to know. Nineteenth floor, that's the last words I think before I go to sleep. I dream I'm in an elevator that's going up up up so far I think I'm dying. The elevator open and it's the coffee-cream-colored man from Spanish talk land. I recognize him from when I was having my baby bleeding on the kitchen floor. He put his hand on my forehead again and whisper, "Push, Precious, you gonna hafta *push*."


Precious woke up remembering not the dream but the last time she had pushed. It was two whole days before they brought the baby to her, and she got to see just what "a little trouble breathing" meant. She tried to hold out her arms but she was more tired than she had ever been in her life. The butter-colored nurse and a little black nurse were standing there by her bed. The little black nurse was holding the baby. Nurse Butter reached under the covers and took Precious' hands, which were balled in fists, and unclenched them, running her own fingers soothingly over Precious' palms. Then she looked the other nurse in the eye. The little black nurse went to hand the baby to Precious but Nurse Butter jumped up and took the baby from her.

"Something is wrong with your baby," she whispered, "but she's alive. She's yours." Nurse Butter laid the blanket-swathed infant in Precious' arms. Precious peered deeply into the slanted eyes and at the flat face with the tongue thrusting in and out.

"Mongoloid," the other nurse said. Nurse Butter cut her eyes at her.

"What happened?" Precious asked dully.

"Well, a lot of things. The doctor will talk in more depth with you, Ms Jones. It looks like your baby may have Down's syndrome and have suffered some oxygen deprivation at birth. Plus you're so young, things happen more to the very young—" Her voice trailed off for a second. "Did you see a doctor at all while you were pregnant?"

Precious didn't answer her. She lifted up her arms and held out the baby to Nurse Butter. Nurse Butter nodded to the little black nurse, who took the baby away. Nurse Butter hiked herself up on the side of the bed. She was trying to get her arms around Precious. She stroked her forehead and told her, "I'm so sorry, Ms Jones, so sorry."

Precious tried to turn away from her but the butter-colored nurse from Greenwood, Mississippi, held her tighter, pulling Precious' chest and shoulders into her arms. Precious could smell her lotion-starch-deodorant-uniform smell and the faint odor of Juicy Fruit chewing gum and she could feel a warmth coming from her she had never felt from her mother. And she began to cry. A little at first, then on and on, *everything* hurt—the bloody tear between her legs, the big black-blue on the side of her head where her mother had kicked her but Nurse Butter didn't see it and was holding her too tight there. Precious heaved and sobbed for the flat-faced child, for herself that had never been held before. Even her father who came to her in the night had not held her but had pushed her back and flung his stinky pee-pee smelling thing in her mouth, then finally in her vagina. Years and years like that. First grade had started in a dirty pink dress that had his smell smeared on it. Second grade. Third grade. Fourth grade. It seemed like the night was his and she was part of it. Invisible dark disappeared. It was so dark she had just stopped—stopped talking, bouncing the ball, filling in between the dotted lines, identifying shapes and colors. What difference did it make whether the purple blob was a square or a circle. Whether it was blue or purple or yellow for that matter.

What difference did it make which way the letters pointed on the page, whether the roof of the gingerbread house faced the top or the bottom of the page. Precious put the book, doll, jump rope, her head, self, down, very quietly, in the back of the class when she was six years old. She hadn't really looked up again until she was twelve and the EMS man had asked her to when he found her moaning on the kitchen floor at 444 Lenox Avenue, and now this nurse was holding her face telling her, "Look at me sweetie, you gonna get through this. You really are gonna get through this."

Precious looked up at her in pained bewilderment, remembering her mother's shoe coming like a bullet to the side of her head, her father's penis dangling in her face, and now the flat-face baby with eyes like Koreans.

"How?" she cried. "How?"

The baby went to live over on 150th and St Nicholas Avenue with her grandmother, Precious' mother's mother, even though her mother had told the welfare the baby live with her and Precious, and that she take care of it while Precious go to school.

About three months after the baby was born, Precious still twelve years old, Precious' mother slap her. HARD. Then she pick up the cast-iron skillet, thank god it was no hot grease in it, and hit Precious so hard on her back she fall on floor. Then she kick Precious in the ribs. Then she say, "Thank you Miz Claireece Precious Jones for fucking my husband you nasty little slut!" Precious felt like she was gonna die. She couldn't breathe, from where she had baby start to hurt.

"Fat cunt bucket slut! Nigger pig bitch! He done quit me! He done left me 'cause of you! What you tell them mutherfuckers at the damn hospital? I should KILL you!" she bellowed.

Precious lay on the floor shaking, crying, scared her mother was gonna kill her. "Get up Miss Hot-to-Trot," her mother shouted. "Git your Jezebel ass up and fix some dinner 'fore I give you something to cry about." Precious got up from the floor and fixed dinner. She fixed collard greens and ham hocks, corn bread, fried apple pies, and macaroni 'n cheese. She was in the kitchen two hours. Precious knew two hours had passed even if she couldn't look at the clock and tell it. The man on the radio say four o'clock, tell some news, music, by the time she's fixing her mother's plate man say six o'clock. Her neck, shoulder, and back felt like cars were rolling over them. She carried her mother a plate which she set it in front of her on a TV tray.

"Where's yours?" her mother demanded staring at her.

"I'm not hongry."

Devil red sparks flashed in her mother's eyes and the big crease in her forehead deepened.

"I . . . my shoulder hurt . . . I wanna lay down."

"Ain' nothin' wrong with your shoulder, I barely

touched you! Go get a plate and stop acting stupid 'fore
I do hurt your shoulder."

Precious went back to the kitchen and fixed herself a
plate. "Margarine!" her mother hollered. "Bring me
some margarine and the hot sauce." Precious brought
the margarine and the hot sauce, then returned to the
kitchen to pile on her own plate the dark bittersweet
greens, ham hocks, macaroni 'n cheese, fried pies, and
corn bread dripping with margarine. She ate silently,
relentlessly, unable to taste anything because of the
purple throbbing in her back and shoulder, and the
white sharp pain shooting up her neck.

Some white people was smiling and kissing on televi-
sion. "Oh ain't he cute!" her mother moaned over a black
actor in a beer commercial. She pushed her plate toward
Precious. "Get me some more. Get you some—"

"I don't want no more."

"Did you hear me?"

Precious got up and took her and her mother's plate
back to the kitchen. She was so full she felt she would
bust. She looked over at her mother, her greasy lips, her
brown face swollen like a grotesque pumpkin, her torn
flowered housedress, her dark brown thighs spreading
out from under the torn shift. Precious got scared looking at her mother. If Precious was fat, there was no
word to describe her mother, who took up half the
couch, whose arms seemed like huge animals. She set
her mother's plate in front of her. "Ain' no more pies?"

"There is," Precious answered.

"Bring me a few when you bring back your plate, hurry up stupid 'fore I kick your ass!"

Precious shuffled back into the living room, her own plate piled higher than it had been the first time. She did this because she knew her mother would just make her go back to the kitchen and get more. She set a bowl with the rest of the little fried pies on her mother's tray and she sat down and ate. Ate watching the grease run down her mother's chin. Ate watching her mother grab a whole ham hock wif her hand, then watched herself do the same thing, felt the slick fat meat explode its salty lusty taste in her mouth, the macaroni 'n cheese, the greens. She ate fixedly, pointedly, moving from meat to macaroni to greens to the fried pies. The purple pain in her back and shoulders did not go away, neither did the white sharp pain shooting through her neck, but it mattered less. She was at the point in drowning when water had filled the lungs and the fight for air is over and death is a second away. She fell back on the sofa in a stupor but the pain in her shoulder was so bad she did not fall asleep like she usually did after she had been forced to eat by her mother. Her eyes closed. She felt her mother's hand between her thighs. She stirred, felt her mother's strong fingers and thumb gather into a pinch. She stopped moving and fell back further into the couch as if she was asleep. She didn't have to open her eyes, she knew by the smell in the room her mother's hand was between her own legs. Her mother had stopped being able to fit in the bathtub a long time ago. Her mother's hand inched up Precious' thighs into the wet opening of her vagina. Precious fell for real now into the sleep she had been faking.

She is twelve, no *was* twelve? She is sixteen now. For the past couple of weeks or so, ever since white bitch Lichenstein kick her outta school, 1983 and 1987, twelve years old and sixteen years old, the first baby and this one coming, all been getting mixed up in her head. Did her mother just hit her with the iron skillet? Was the ache in her shoulder old or new? The baby, new-born and wrapped in white blankets, or dead eyed, fat, and lying in crib at her grandmother's? Time seemed like clothes in the washing machine at laundry mat— round 'n round, up 'n down. One minute she was a little girl twelve years old being kicked in the head by Mama, the next she was jumping over the desk on Mrs Lichenstein's ass. Precious pushed up from the sofa and looked at her mother who was asleep. It was Friday, October 16, 1987. She had to get through Saturday and Sunday before she got to Monday—the *alternative*.

*School?* She should go down to the welfare, her mother said, school couldn't help her none *now*. Precious pulled on a pair of neon yellow leggings and her beige X sweatshirt. She put on her white Reeboks, balled up two one-dollar bills and stuck them in her bra, rubbed some petroleum jelly on her face, patted her hair promising herself soon as she got some money she would get some braids. She looked away from the mirror which was sitting on top the white chest of drawers she had had ever since she was a little girl to the single bed of the same white painted wood. On the wall at the foot of the bed was a very big picture of Louis Farrakhan, in bold black letters under the picture was written THE BLACK MAN'S TIME. The red numerals of the clock radio glowed 8:30 a.m. at her. Her mother was sleep. She wouldn't be gone that long. She'd be back in time to clean up and fix breakfast for her mother. Precious had asked her mother once, How come you never do anything? When she had got up off the floor her mother had told her, 'Cause that's what you here for.

I is goin' down to the nineteenth floor of the Hotel Theresa to the *alternative*, she told herself tying the laces of her Reeboks. She slipped on her green leather jacket and dropped her house keys into the pocket. I is going. She walked out her room to the front door.

"Where you going?" Mama's voice shot out from her bedroom.

Why wasn't her fat ass sleep? Precious didn't answer her. "You hear me talkin' to you!" Precious started undoing the four locks on the front door. "Precious!" Fuck you bitch. Ize gone! She giggled as she moved as fast as she could being pregnant and all. The staircase was so narrow both sides of her were touching some part of the building as she walked down the stairs. Maybe after I have baby I lose some weight. Maybe I get my own place.

When she stepped out in the morning Lenox Avenue was alive with cars and gypsy cabs and buses. Delivery trucks were parked in front of the supermarket and the McDonald's on the corner of 132nd. Men, women, and children were crowded at bus stops on their way downtown to school and work. Wonder where they go to work, she mused as she walked down Lenox Avenue, where I gonna go to work. How I'm gonna get out HER house? I hate her. Precious stopped at the light on 126th Street and looked across the street at Sylvia's then down the block at the African vendors lining the street selling Kente cloth, cowrie shell earrings and necklaces, leather belts and purses.

She was walking slow slow now. No one said anything to her. Boys and men that would have hooted and howled at her "Hey Baby! All that meat and no potatoes!" or "Hey Big Mama!" were silent now that her belly was stuck out a foot in front of her. She was safe. Safe from the men on the street, she thought, but was she safe from him, Carl Jones? This is my second baby for my fahver, it gonna be retarded too?

This time she knew Mama knew. Umm hmm, she knew. She brought him to me. I ain' crazy, that stinky hoe give me to him. Thas what he require to fuck her

probably, some of me. He had gotten to where he jus'
climb on her. "Shut up!" he say. "You wide as the
Mississippi," he howled, slapping her ass, "don't tell me
a little bit of dick hurt you heifer. Git usta it." He laffed.
"You *is* usta it." Precious laid back on the bed while he
fell on top of her. She see herself dancing in videos, in
the movies; she be breaking, *fly*, just a dancing, maybe,
no! not maybe—she out there! Umm hmm heating up
the stage at the Apollo for Doug E. Fresh or Al B.
Shure. They love her, say she one of the best dancers,
ain' no doubt of, or about, that!

I gonna marry you, he be saying. Hurry up nigger,
shut up! He mess up her dream talking and grunting.
First he mess up her life fucking her, then he mess up
the fucking by talking stupid shit. The fucking embarrass her. Oh shut up! Nigger, how you gonna marry me
and you is my daddy, she wanna shout. I'm your daughter, fucking me illegal. But she keep her mouth shut so's
the fuckin' don't turn into a beating. It start to feel
good. Her body stop being a video dancer and start
coming. She try to pull herself back to dancing on the
video but she rocking under Carl now, her twat jumping juicy, it feel good. She feel 'shamed. *See, see,* he slap
her thigh like cowboys on TV do horses, then he
squeeze her nipple, bite down on it. She come some
more. He slap her thigh, *See,* you *LIKE* it! You like your
mama—you die for it! He pull his dick out her, the
warm white come pour out her hole damping up the
sheets.

She is leaning against the glass partition of the bus stop on 125th Street.

"Are you getting on the bus young lady?"

Precious blinks at the bus driver and shakes her head no. She looks bewildered at the disappearing 101 bus. She doesn't remember walking to the bus stop and up under its glass shelter. She doesn't even remember what she doing out the house until she looks down at her neon yellow leggings and white Reeboks, of course! Alternative. She on her, *was* on her way, walking down Lenox 'bout to hit one-two-five then bad thoughts hit her 'n she space out.

"You OK?" guy in a uniform for like working in a garage ask her.

"I'm OK, I'm OK," she protested brushing the people off who had gathered around to help her.

"That bitch crazy man!" a skinny dude in baggies said real loud to a tall boy next to him.

"Fuck you narrow behind mutherfucker! Mind your bizness!" Precious screamed as she barreled down 125th Street toward the Hotel Theresa looming up from Adam Clayton Powell Jr Blvd like a tall ivory face with hundreds of square dark windows for eyes. She crosses 125th and heads for the hotel. She has passed it a hundred times but never been in it. She walks through the front door, past a man at a desk, to the black doors of the hotel's two elevators. The doors open. She steps inside, no one is in the elevator but her. It's not going anywhere. Oh, she pushes the button.

She steps out the elevator and sees a tan-colored woman with glasses and cornrowed hair sitting at a black desk next to a door with a sign with black letters on it.

"This the alternative?" Precious asks.

"The *what?*" the woman says raising her eyebrows and peering over the top of her glasses at Precious.

"This the alternative?" she repeated getting kinda mad—that bitch heard her!

"What exactly are you looking for?" the woman said soothingly.

"Well, what is this here?"

"This is Higher Education Alternative/Each One Teach One."

"I'm looking for alternative school."

"Well," woman peered at her some more, "this *is* an alternative school."

Precious had never seen anybody with braids that didn't hang down before. Why get 'em put in if you wasn't going to get extensions.

"What alternative is?" Mayest wellst gone ask the bitch, fine out now what kinda school this gonna be.

"I don't know if I understand what you're asking me?"

"Alternative—lady from my other school tell me to come here to Hotel Theresa, nineteenth floor, it's *alternative* school."

"OK, OK," the woman said, "Each One Teach One

is an alternative school and an alternative is like a choice, a different way to do something."

"Oh."

"What school did you come from?"

"From I.S. 146."

"That's a junior high school isn't it?"

"I'm sixteen."

"You need discharge papers from your old school saying they have formally discharged you or we can't allow you in the program."

"I got kicked out 'cause I'm pregnant—"

"Yes, yes, I understand but you still need formal discharge papers or we can't let you in. It's the law."

"Mrs Lichenstein ain' say all that."

"Oh you're the one Mrs Lichenstein called about."

"She call?" Precious say surprised.

"Yes, yes," she murmured, "said to be on the lookout for you, you might be coming our way." She fumbled with some papers on her desk. "Claireece P. Jones?"

"Thas me." Precious was pleased. She didn't ever remember anyone being on the lookout for her before. Yeah, lookout see if she was gonna steal something or some shit but not look to see if she coming. That was nice.

"Well the principal at I.S. 146 already sent your discharge papers and stuff over."

"What stuff?"

"Your academic record—" The woman stopped

bewildered by the expression on Precious' face. "Are you all right?"

"They done sent my file!" Precious spat out the word "file."

"Well, we had to have ahh certain information before we could accept you into the program. Our students have to meet certain income, residential, and academic requirements before we can let them in. Their sending your records over was just a way of speeding things up for you."

Precious wondered what file said. She knew file said she had a baby. Did file say who daddy. What kinda baby? Did file say how pages don't mean much to her, how much she weigh, how many fights she had? What file say? She couldn't read file but she know every time they wants to fuck with her or decide her life—here they come with the mutherfucking file. Well, OK, they got file, know every mutherfucking thing. So, what's the big deal, let's get it on.

"Can I start today?" Precious ask, demand actually, she demanding (since they know so much).

"Well of course," Cornrows say, "I mean we have an entry procedure but most of that has actually been completed for you. The only thing we really need is income verification. Are you currently receiving AFDC?"

"No."

Cornrows raise her eyebrows.

"My muver get AFDC for me and my daughter."

"Oh, you've had an amniocentesis?" the woman asked peering over her glasses at Precious' belly now.

"Huh?"

"You said your mother was receiving a check for you and your daughter?" She nodded to Precious' stomach.

"Not this baby! I got another baby 'sides this one coming."

"Oh, I see. So your mother has custody of you and your daughter. In other words you're on her 'budget.'"

"Umm hmm." Precious nod yes, this bitch ain' no dummy.

"OK, well I need a copy of your mother's budget, and a current phone or utilities bill, OK?"

"OK." Precious stare at her hard. "I got to go get all that *now*?"

"No, no, relax, we're gonna give you a few tests; test your reading and math level, see whether to put you in pre-G.E.D. or G.E.D."

"What's the difference?"

"Well G.E.D. classes are for students whose basic skills are up to par and they're ready to just go into a class and start working on their G.E.D. Pre-G.E.D. is when the student needs some work to get up to the level of the G.E.D. class."

"What level that?"

"Well, to enter G.E.D. classes a student should be able to read on an eighth-grade level. They should score 8.0 or better on the TABE reading test."

"I was in the ninfe grade at I.S. 146."

"Then you should have no problem," the cornrow head woman said smiling.

"What's the problem?" I axes the fat dark-skin woman who is looking over my shoulder at my answer sheet. She got leggings like mine 'cept hers black. She got on blue blouse, look nice, like silk. She look OK I guess. I like light-skin people, they nice. I likes slim people too. Mama fat black, if I weigh two hundred she weigh three. The fat lady is looking at me. I looks back, she ain' answered my question.

"What's the problem?" I axes again.

"Well I think maybe you may need to take the test again—"

"You the teacher?"

"One of them."

"What you teach?"

"I teach the G.E.D. class."

"Who the other teacher?"

"Ms Rain."

"What she teach?"

"Ms Rain teaches the pre-G.E.D. reading class."

I know thas where I b'long, "Thas where I b'long," I tell her.

"Hmmm," go fat black heifer and look at me. I don't believe this bitch no teacher.

"Do you want to take the test again?"

"No."

For me this nuffin' new. There has always been something wrong wif the tesses. The tesses paint a picture of me wif no brain. The tesses paint a picture of me an' my muver—my whole family, we more than dumb, we invisible. One time I seen us on TV. It was a show of spooky shit, an' castles, you know shit be all haunted. And the peoples, well some of them was peoples and some of them was vampire peoples. But the real peoples did not know it till it was party time. You know crackers eating roast turkey and champagne and shit. So it's five of 'em sitting on the couch; and one of 'em git up and take a picture. Got it? When picture develop (it's insta-matic) only *one* person on the couch. The other peoples did not exist. They vampires. They eats, drinks, wear clothes, talks, fucks, and stuff but when you git right down to it they don't exist.

I big, I talk, I eats, I cooks, I laugh, watch TV, do what my muver say. But I can see when the picture come back I don't exist. Don't nobody want me. Don't nobody need me. I know who I am. I know who they say I am—vampire sucking the system's blood. Ugly black grease to be wipe away, punish, kilt, changed, finded a job for.

I wanna say I am somebody. I wanna say it on subway, TV, movie, LOUD. I see the pink faces in suits look over top of my head. I watch myself disappear in their eyes, their tesses. I talk loud but still I don't exist.

I see it over and over, the real people, the people who show up when the picture come back; and they are pritty people, girls with little titties like buttons and legs like long white straws. Do all white people look like pictures? No, 'cause the white people at school is fat and cruel like evil witches from fairy tales but they exist. Is it because they white? If Mrs Lichenstein who have elephant stomach and garbage smell from her pussy exist, why don't I? Why can't I see myself, *feel* where I end and begin. I sometimes look in the pink people in suits eyes, the men from bizness, and they look way above me, put me out of their eyes. My fahver don't see me really. If he did he would know I was like a white girl, a *real* person, inside. He would not climb on me from forever and stick his dick in me 'n get me inside on fire, bleed, I bleed then he slap me. Can't he see I am a girl for flowers and thin straw legs and a place in the picture. I been out the picture so long I am used to it. But that don't mean it don't hurt. Sometimes I pass by store window and somebody fat dark skin, old looking, someone look like my muver look back at me. But I know it can't be my muver 'cause my muver is at home. She have not left home since Little Mongo was born. Who I see? I stand in tub sometime, look my body, it stretch marks, ripples. I try to hide myself, then I try to show myself. I ax my muver for money to git my hair done, clothes. I know the money she got for me—from my baby. She usta give me money; now every time I ax for money she say I took her husband, her man. Her man? Please! Thas my mutherfuckin' fahver! I hear her tell someone on phone I am heifer, take her husband, I'm fast. What it take for my muver to see me? Sometimes I wish I was not alive. But I don't know how to die. Ain' no plug to pull out. 'N no matter how bad I feel my heart don't stop beating and my eyes open in the morning. I hardly have not seen my daughter since she was a little baby. I never stick my bresses in her mouth. My muver say what for? It's outta style. She say I never do you. What that child of yours need tittie for? She retarded. Mongoloid. Down Sinder.

What tess say? I don't give a fuck. I look bitch teacher woman in face, trying to see do she see *me* or the tess. But I don't care now what anybody see. I see something, somebody. I got baby. So what. I feel proud 'cept it's baby by my fahver and that make me not in picture again.

*"Again?"*

Is she saying something? It's teacher woman, "Would you like to take the test again?"

I shake my head no. What for, it gonna be the same, I ain't change. I still me, Precious. She say I in first class which meet Monday, Wednesday, and Friday, 9 a.m. to 12 noon. I say, "I usta going to school everyday all day." She asks me if I could get use to something else. I don't say nuffin', then I say loud, "YES."

■

First thing I see when I wake up is picture of Farrakhan's face on the wall. I love him. He is against crack addicts and crackers. Crackers is the cause of everything bad. It why my father ack like he do. He has forgot he is the Original Man! So he fuck me, fuck me, beat me, have a chile by me. When he see I'm pregnant the first time he disappear. I think for years, for a long time I know that much.

After my baby and me come out of the hospital my muver take us down to welfare; say I is mother but just a chile and she taking care of bofe us'es. So really all she did was add my baby to her budget. She already on the 'fare wit' me so she just add my daughter. I could be on the 'fare for myself now, I think. I'm old enuff. I'm 16. But I'm not sure I know how to be on my own. I have to say sometimes I hate my muver. She don't love me. I wonder how she could love Little Mongo (thas my daughter. Mongo sound Spanish don't it? Yeah, thas why I chose it, but what it is is short for Mongoloid Down Sinder, which is what she is; sometimes what I feel I is. I feel so stupid sometimes. So ugly, worth nuffin'. I could just sit here wif my muver everyday wif the shades drawed, watching TV, eat, watch TV, eat. Carl come over fuck us'es. Go from room to room, slap me on my ass when he through, holler WHEEE WHEEE! Call me name Butter Ball Big Mama Two Ton of Fun. I hate hear him talk more than I hate fuck. Sometimes fuck feel good. That confuse me, everything get swimming for me, floating like for days sometimes. I just sit in back classroom, somebody say something I shout on 'em, hit 'em; rest of the time I mine my bizness. I was on my way to graduate from I.S. 146 'n then fuckface Miz Lichenstein mess shit up. I . . . , in my inside world, I am so pretty, like a advertisement girl on commercial, 'n some-one ride up here in car, someone look like the son of that guy that got kilt when he was president a long time ago or Tom Cruise—or anybody like that pull up here in a car and I be riding like on TV chile—JeeZUS! It's 8 a.m. o'clock! I know I woketed up at 6 a.m., lord where the time go! I got to get dress for school. I got to be at school by 9 a.m. Today is first day. I been tessed. I been incomed eligible. I got Medicaid card and proof of address. All that shit. I is ready. Ready for school. School something (this *nuthin'*!). School gonna help me get out dis house. I gotta throw some water on my ass and git up. What I'm gonna wear what I'm gonna wear? One thing I do got is clothes, thanks to my muver's charge at Lane Bryant 'n man sell hot shit. Come to building go from door to door, I got your size he call out in hallway I got your size. I got to get dress. I wear my pink stretch pants? I think so, wif my black pesint blouse. I go splash some water on my ass, which mean I wash serious between my legs and underarm. I don't smell like my muver. I *don't*. I ain' got no money for lunch or McDonald's for breakfast. I take piece of ham out frigidare, wrap it in aluminum foil, I'll eat it walking down Lenox, not as good as Egg McMuffin but beat nuffin'. I double back to my room. On top my dresser is notebook. Ol' Cornrows say bring self, pencil, and notebook. I got self, pencil, and notebook. Can I get a witness! I'm outta here!

I always did like school, jus' seem school never did like me. Kinnergarden and first grade I don't talk, they laff at that. Second grade my cherry busted. I don't want to think that now. I look across the street at McDonald's but I ain't got no money so I unwrap ham and take a bite. I'm gonna ask Mama for some money when she get her check, plus the school gonna give me a stipend, thas money for goin' to school. Secon' grade they laffes at HOW I talk. So I stop talking. What for? Secon' thas when the "I'mma joke" start. When I go sit down boyz make fart sounds wif they mouf like it's me fartin'. When I git up they snort snort hog grunt sounds. So I jus' stop getting up. What for? Thas when I start to pee on myself. I just sit there, it's like I paralyze or some shit. I don't move. I *can't* move. Secon' grade teacher HATE me. Oh that woman hate me. I look at myself in the window of the fried chicken joint between 127th and 126th. I look good in my pink stretch pants. Woman at Lane Bryant on one-two-five say no reason big girls can't wear the latest, so I wear it. But boyz still laff me, what could I wear that boyz don't laff? Secon' grade is when I just start to sit there. All day. Other kids run all around. Me, Claireece P. Jones, come in 8:55 a.m., sit down, don't move till the bell ring to go home. I wet myself. Don't know why I don't get up, but I don't. I jus' sit there and pee. Teacher ack all care at first, then scream, then get Principal. Principal call Mama and who else I don't remember. Finally Principal say, Let it be. Be glad thas all the trouble she give you. Focus on the ones who *can* learn, Principal say to teacher. What that mean? Is she one of the ones who can't?

My head hurt. I gotta eat something. It's 8:45 a.m. I gotta be at school at 9 a.m. Ham gone. I ain't got no money. I turn back to chicken place. Walk in cool tell lady, Give me a basket. Chicken look like last night's but people in there buying it ol' or not. Lady ax, Fries? I say, Potato salad. Potato salad in the refrigerator in the back. I know that. Lady turn roun' to go in back, I grab chicken and roll, turn, run out, and cut down one-two-six stuffing chicken in my mouth. "Scarf Big Mama!" this from crack addict standing in front abandoned building. I don't even turn my head—crack addicts is *disgusting*! Give race a bad name, lost in the hells of norf america crack addicts is.

I look at watch, 8:57 a.m.! But shit I'm almost there! Coming around the corner of 126th onto Adam Clayton Powell Jr Blvd. I throws the chicken bones into the trash can on the corner, wipe the grease off my mouth with the roll then stuff rest of roll in my mouf, run across 125th, and I'm there! I'm in the elevator moving up when I realize I left my notebook and pencil in the chicken place! Goddam! And it's 9:05 a.m. not 9:00 a.m. Oh well teacher nigger too. Don't care if she teacher, don't no niggers start on time. The elevator goes Bing! I step out. My class last door on left. My teacher Miz Rain.


I'm walking across the lobby room real real slow. Full of chicken, bread; usually that make me not want to cry remember, but I feel like crying now. My head is like the swimming pool at the Y on one-three-five. Summer full of bodies splashing, most in shallow end; one, two in deep end. Thas how all the time years is swimming in my head. First grade boy say, Pick up your lips Claireece 'fore you trip over them. Call me shoe shine shinola. Second grade I is fat. Thas when fart sounds and pig grunt sounds start. No boyfriend no girlfriends. I stare at the blackboard pretending. I don't know what I'm pretending—that trains ain' riding through my head sometime and that yes, I'm reading along with the class on page 55 of the reader. Early on I realize no one hear the TV set voices growing out blackboard but me, so I try not to answer them. Over in deepest end of the pool (where you could drown if not for fine lifeguard look like Bobby Brown) is me sitting in my chair at my desk and the world turn to whirring sound, everything is noise, teacher's voice white static. My pee pee open hot stinky down my thighs sssssss splatter splatter. I wanna die I hate myself HATE myself. Giggles giggles but I don't move I barely breathe I just sit. They giggle. I stare straight ahead. They talk me. I don't say nuffin'.

Seven, he on me almost every night. First it's just in my mouth. Then it's more more. He is intercoursing me. Say I can take it. Look you don't even bleed, virgin girls bleed. You not virgin. I'm *seven*.

I don't realize I've gone from walking real real slow to standing perfectly still. I'm in the lobby of first day of school Higher Education Alternative/Each One Teach One just standing there. I realize this 'cause Miz Rain done peeked her head out last door on the left and said, "You alright?" I know who she is 'cause Miss Cornrow with the glasses had done pointed her out to me after I finish testing and show me my teacher and classroom.

I make my feet move. I don't say anything. Nothing in my mouth to say. I move my feet some more. Miz Rain ask me if I'm in the A.B.E. class. I say yes. She say this is it and go back inside door. The first thing I see when I step through door is the windows, where we is is high up, no other buildings in the way. Sky blue blue. I looks around the room now. Walls painted lite ugly green. Miz Rain at her desk, her back to me, her face to the class and the windows. "Class" only about five, six other people. Miz Teacher turn around say, Have a seat. I stays standing at door. I swallow hard, start to, I think I'm gonna cry. I look Miz Teacher's long dreadlocky hair, look kinda nice but look kinda nasty too. My knees is shaking, I'm scared I'm gonna pee on myself, even though I has not done no shit like that in years. I don't know how I'm gonna do it, but I am—I look at the six chairs line up neat in the back of the room. I gotta get there.

The whole class quiet. Everybody staring at me. God don't let me cry. I takes in air through my nose, a big big breath, then I start to walk slow to the back. But something like birds or light fly through my heart. An' my feet stop. At the first row. An' for the first time in my life I sits down in the front row (which is good 'cause I never could see the board from the back).

I ain' got no notebook, no money. My head is big 'lympic size pool, all the years, all the me's floating around glued shamed to desks while pee puddles get big near their feet. Man don't nobody know it but it ain' no joke for me to be here in this school. I glance above teacher's head at the wall. Is a picture of small dark lady with face like prune and dress from the oldern days. I wonder who she is. Teacher sit at desk marking roll sheet, got on purple dress and running shoes. She dark, got nice face, big eyes, and hair like I already said. My muver do not like niggers wear they hair like that! My muver say Farrakhan OK but he done gone too far. Too far where I wanna ax. I don't know how *I* feel about people with hair like that.

The teacher is talking.

"You'll need a notebook like this," she hold up a black 'n white 79-cent notebook just like what I left in chicken place. As she talking girl walk in.

"It's nine thirty-seven," teacher say. "Jo Ann you *late*."

"I had to stop and get something to eat."

"Next time stay where you stop. Starting tomorrow this door will be locked at nine o'clock!"

"I better be on the side that's in," grumble Jo Ann.

"We agree on that," say teacher, she look Jo Ann in eye. She not scared of Jo Ann. Well gone Miz Rain.

"We got some new people—"

"I found something!" Jo Ann shout.

"I beg your pardon," say teacher but you can see she ain' beggin' nothin', she mad.

"No, I'm sorry Ms Rain"—I see right now Jo Ann is clown—"but I jus' want to say, do anyone need an extra notebook I foun' in the chicken place?"

"It's mine!" I say.

"Git a grip," Jo Ann say.

"I got one." I shocks myself saying that. "I left that book at Arkansas Jr. Fried Chicken on Lenox between one-two-seven and one-two-six this morning."

"Well I'll be a turkey's asshole!" Jo Ann screamed. "Thas where I found it."

I reaches my hand she smile me. Han' me my book, look at my stomach, say, "When you due?"

I say, "Not sure."

She frown, don't say nothing, and go sit a couple seats away from me in the row right behind me.

Miz Rain look pretty bent out of shape then melt, say, "We got more new people than old people today, so let's just go back to day one and git to know each other and figure out what we gonna do here together." I look at her weird. Ain' she spozed to *know* what we gonna do. How we gonna figure anything out. Weze ignerent. We here to learn, leas' I am. God I hope this don't be another . . . another . . . I don't know—another like before, yeah another like the years before.

"Let's try a circle," teacher say. Damn I just did sit myself down in front row and now we getting in a circle.

"We don't need all those chairs," teacher say waving at Jo Ann who dragging chairs from second row. "Just pull out five or six, however many of us it is, and put 'em in a little circle and then we'll put 'em back in rows after we finish introducing ourselves." She sit herself in one of the chairs and we all do the same (I mean she the teacher 'n all).

"OK," she say, "let's get to know each other a little bit uummm, let's see, how about your name, where you were born, your favorite color, and something you do good and why you're here."

"Huh?" Big red girl snort. Miss Rain go to board and say, "Number one, your name," then she write it, "number two, where you were born," and so on until it all on board:

1. name
2. where you were born
3. favorite color
4. something you do good
5. why you are here today

She sit back down say, "OK, I'll start. My name is Blue Rain—"

"Thas your real name!" This from girl with boy suit on.

"Um hmmm, that's my for real hope to die if I'm lying name."

"Your first name *Blue*?" same girl say.

"Um hmm," Ms Rain say this like she tired of mannish girl.

"Splain that!"

"Well," say Ms Rain real proper. "I don't feel I have to explain my name." She look at girl, girl git message. "Now as I was saying my name is Blue Rain. I was born in California. My favorite color is purple. What do I do good? Ummm, I sing purty good. And I'm here because my girlfriend used to teach here and she was out one day and asked me to substitute for her, then when she quit, they asked me did I want the job. I said yeah and I been here ever since."

I look around the circle, it's six people, not counting me. A big redbone girl, loud bug-out girl who find my notebook at chicken place, Spanish girl with light skin, then this brown-skin Spanish girl, and a girl my color in boy suit, look like some kinda butch.

Big Red talking now, "My name Rhonda Patrice Johnson." Rhonda big, taller than me, light skin but it don't do nuffin' for her. She ugly, got big lips, pig nose, she fat fat and her hair rusty color but short short.

"I was born in Kingston, Jamaica." Ain' that something! She don't talk funny at all like how coconut head peoples do. "My favorite color is blue, I cook good."

"What?" somebody say.

"Name it!" Rhonda shoot back.

"Peas 'n rice!"

"Yeah yeah," like why even mention somethin' so basic.

"Curry goat!"

"Yeah, you name it," Rhonda say. "My mother usta have a restaurant on Seventh Ave before she got sick, she taught me everything. I'm here," she say serious, "to bring my reading up so I could get my G.E.D."

The skinny light-skin Spanish girl speak, "My name is Rita Romero. I was born right here in Harlem. I'm here because I was an addict and dropped out of school and never got my reading and writing together. My favorite color is black." She smile messed up teef. "I guess you could tell that." We could looking at her clothes 'n shoes, all black.

"What you do good?" Rhonda ax.

"Hmm," she say, then in shaky voice real slow, "I'm a good mother, a very good mother."

Brown girl talk. We about the same color but I think thas all we got the same. I is *all* girl. Don't know here.

"My name is Jermaine."

Uh oh! Some kinda freak.

"My favorite color—"

"Tell us where you born first," Rhonda again.

Jermaine give Rhonda a piss on you look. Rhonda

cut her eyes at Jermaine like jump bad if you want to. Jermaine say she was born in the Bronx, still live there. Red her favorite color. She a good dancer. She come here 'cause she want to get away from negative influence of the Bronx.

Spanish girl Rita say, "You come to *Harlem* to get away from bad influence?"

Jermaine, which I don't have to tell you is a *boy's* name, say, "It's *who* you know and I know too many people in the Bronx baby."

"How did you find out about the program?" Miz Rain ax.

"A friend."

Miz Rain don't say nothin' else.

Girl foun' my notebook next. "Jo Ann is my name, rap is my game. My color is beige. My ambition is to have my own record layer."

Miz Rain look at her. I wonder myself what is a record layer.

"Where was you born and why you at this school," Rhonda ax. OK, I see Rhonda like to run things.

"I was born in King's County Hospital. My mother moved us to Harlem when I was nine years old. I'm here to get my G.E.D., then, well I'm already into the music industry. I just need to take care of the education thing so I can move on up."

Next girl speaks. "My name is Consuelo Montene-gro." Ooohhh she pretty Spanish girl, coffee-cream color wit long ol' good hair. Red blouse. "Why I'm here, favorite color—what's-alla dat shit?" She look Ms Rain in face, mad.

Miz Rain calm. Rain, nice name for her. Ack like she don't mind cursing, say, "It's just a way of breaking the ice, a way of getting to know each other better, by asking nonthreatening questions that allow you to share yourself with a group without having to reveal more of yourself than might be comfortable." She pause. "You don't have to do it if you don't want to."

"I don't want to," beautiful girl say.

Everybody looking at me now. In circle I see everybody, everybody see me. I wish for back of the class again for a second, then I think never that again, I kill myself first 'fore I let that happen.

"My name Precious Jones. I was born in Harlem. My baby gonna be borned in Harlem. I like what color— yellow, thas fresh. 'N I had a problem at my ol' school so I come here."

"Something you do good," Rhonda say.

"Nuffin'," I say.

"Everybody do something good," Ms Rain say in soft voice.

I shake my head, can't think of nuffin'. I'm staring at my shoes.

"One thing," Ms Rain.

"I can cook," I say. I keep my eyes on shoes. I never talk in class before 'cept to cuss teacher or kids if they fuck wif me.

Miz Rain talking about the class. "Periodically we'll be getting into a circle to talk and work but let's put our chairs back in rows for now and move on with our business. Well, first thing, this is a basic reading and writing class, a pre-G.E.D. adult literacy class, a class for beginning readers and writers. This is *not* a G.E.D. class—"

"This not G.E.D.?" Jermaine ax.

"No, it's not. This class is set up to teach students how to read and write," Miz Rain say.

"Shit I know how to read and write, I want to get my G.E.D.," Jo Ann say.

Miz Rain look tired, "Well then this class isn't for you. And I'd appreciate it if you watch your language, this *is* a school."

"Ain' shit to me—"

"Well then go, Jo Ann, why don't you just tip," Miz Rain seem like, you know, well *leave* bitch.

Spanish girl, Rita, say, "Well this here *is* for me. I can't read or write."

Rhonda come in, "I can a little, but I need help."

Jermaine look unsure.

Miz Rain, "If you think you want to be in the G.E.D. class all you have to do is come back to this room at one p.m. for placement testing." Jermaine don't move. Consuelo look to Jermaine but don't say nuffin'. Jo Ann say she be back at one, fuck this shit! She ain' illiterit. Miz Rain look at me. I'm the only one haven't spoken. I wanna say something but don't know how. I'm not use to talkin', how can I say it? I look Miz Rain. She say, "Well Precious, how about you, do you feel you're in the right place?"

I want to tell her what I always wanted to tell someone, that the pages, 'cept for the ones with pictures, look all the same to me; the back row I'm not in today; how I sit in a chair seven years old all day wifout moving. But I'm not seven years old. But I am crying. I look Miz Rain in the face, tears is coming down my eyes, but I'm not sad or embarrass.

"Is I Miz Rain," I axes, "is I in the right place?"

She hand me a tissue, say, "Yes, Precious, yes."


Miz Rain say class need a break. "BE BACK IN 15 MIN-UTES," she say real loud like a machine talk. I get up with the rest, goes out in the lobby. It's empty 'ceptin' us. The other classes don't be here till 12, Miz Rain say. Rhonda say she goin' to the store, anybody want somethin'? I want somethin' but I ain' got no money. Rita give her 50 cents say get chips, salt 'n vinegar, no salt 'n vinegar get plain. Rhonda look me, say, I got you. I look up in her eye. She smile. I feel like I'm gonna cry again. Everybody gonna think I'm a punk, crying, crying. I'm not used to this. But this what I always want, some friendly niceness. I say I pay you back. She say I know you will, what you want. I say barbecue potato chips. She gone! Rhonda move fast for a big girl.

Consuelo, the beautiful Spanish girl, sigh. "Ain' no

guys in our class." This like you know she los' her welfare check after it jus' been cash or somethin'.

Jermaine say, "Good."

Uh oh! Freaky deaky here. I move a little way from her. I don't want no one getting the wrong idea about *me*.

Back in class Miz Rain is telling us what we gonna do everyday. So she *do* know what's what. I was scared for a minute it be like before. Like before I got A in English and never say nuffin', do nuffin'. I sit in seat. I sit in seat everyday for 55 minutes, chair so far back it touch wall. After first day I don't see hear. I play TV in my mind—switch back 'n forth from TV to music videos where I'm dancing in little clothes, shit, *I'm* little.

"Every day," Miz Rain say, "we gonna read and write in our notebooks."

How we gonna write if we can't read? Shit, how we gonna write if we can't write! I don't remember never doing no writing before. My head spinning I'm scared maybe we, maybe this ain' class for me.

Miz Rain talkin'. She say, Chinese saying, I knew she was crazy—we ain' CHINESE! She real serious now, say, "The longest journey begin with a single step." What the fuck that spozed to mean. This school not *Star Trek*. Rita, Spanish girl, looking at Miz Rain like she done see god. Rhonda sitting straight up in her seat. Jermaine looking out the side of her eyes at Consuelo. Consuelo looking at her nails.

Miz Rain hold up notebook, say, "You going to need

one notebook like this"—like what I aweady got—
"and another notebook—loose-leaf or spiral, to keep
your notes and class work in." Complicated complicated, Chinese journeys, 2 books, write 'n you don't
know how—

Jermaine say, "Where we gonna begin?"

Miz Rain say, "At the beginning," and pick a piece of
chalk out her purse and walk to the board. She write *A*
on the board, she hand the chalk to Jermaine. Jermaine
write *B*. Jermaine hand it to Consuelo, she write *C*.
Consuelo hand it to Rhonda she write *D*. Rhonda hand
it to Rita. Rita take a step and start to cry. Miz Rain say
we all in this together. All us say *E* real loud, Rita go up
'n write *E*, hand me chalk 'n I write *F* and so it go. Then
we sits back down all at once, that make us laff, and Miz
Rain say this is the beginning, there are twenty-six letters in the alphabet, they all have a sound. These letters
make up all the words in our language. Please open
your notebook, write the date, October 19, 1987, then
write the alphabet in your notebook.

After we write the alphabet in our notebook we
recite it out loud together. Miz Rain say go home and
practice saying it 'n saying it. On Wednesday she gonna
ask each one to stand up and deliver. Jermaine say,
"Spoze I know it already?" Miz Rain say, "Then it
should be no problem for you." But I remember Jermaine write *Q* after *O* instead of *P*. I remember that. I
gonna practice. I sure am. Miz Rain say on Wednesday
she gonna talk to us about keeping a journal. Tell us

again we gotta bring in another notebook for to be our journal. How is a journal different from a notebook I wanna ask but I never asked a question before in school.

I feels little music in my head. I know I'm tripping. I feel the baby in my stomach. Don't feel good. I try not to think about my stomach big like this—the heavy pressing down on my bladder parts, like a fucking watermelon under my skin. See a doctor? My muver want me to go get on welfare. But I'm on welfare—hers. It's like you know, I know she ain't gonna get money for me I ain' in school; she gonna always get money for my daughter 'cause she retarded. Maybe somethin' gonna be wrong wif this baby too. I don't care, maybe if new baby Down Sinder I can get my own check.

But I don't know if I want check. I wonder what reading books be like.

Miz Rain say we almost finished for the day, say she wanna spend some time with each student in little office room to side before we go. Say she gonna call us out one by one in alphabetical order. I feel panicking panicking— I don't know alphabetical order—whas that!

Miz Rain say she be in little office, get up, then say unsure like, I never seen teacher unsure ('less you gettin' ready to hit 'em). She say, "Yall can call me Blue if you want." I look her like she crazy—why we want that? I might say some bad things I get mad or somebody fuck with me or somethin', but I try to show *respect* for peoples. So I say to myself, No, Miz Rain, I don't want call you Blue. "Or . . . or," she says, "Rain, some people jus' call me Rain." Her voice got a country soun' to it. Jermaine says, "I like that, Rain." Don' nobody else say nothing.

Rhonda git up after Miz Rain gone. Rhonda something.

"OK, look at alphabets," she say loud. I wanna say you ain' got to talk so loud, but I don't. "OK," she say, "which name go first."

Consuelo say, "I guess that's me." I wanna know why but I don't ask. I see Rhonda somethin' else of a lady. Wifout me axin', she say, "You git it Precious?" I says, "No." She say, "Look at the alphabets—anybody name start wif *A* in here." I shake my head. "*B*?" I shake my head no. "*C*?" Don't shake my head. "Good!" she say. She say, "Consuelo start wif *C*, she first." She write:

1. Consuelo

Who next? she axes me. I don't know. She point to *D, E, F, G*. I look Jermaine. Jermaine say, "My name start wif *J*." Rhonda go, *H, I, J*—
I point Jermaine. Now it's:

1. Consuelo
2. Jermaine

Miz Rain stick head in door. Rhonda say, "Give us five." Miz Rain smile us 'n go back out. Rhonda go, "*K, L, M, N, O, P*—"

"*P* for Precious!" I hollers. "I'm next."
"You got it, you got it," Rhonda say.

1. Consuelo
2. Jermaine
3. Precious

"*Q, R—*"
"Rita!" Thas Rita shout that. "I'm *R* too." Rhonda quiz us, "Which go first me or her?" Jermaine say, "You do," to Rhonda. I don't know why. I remember Jo Ann. I know that *J* like Jermaine. If she wasn't gone where would she go, in front Jermaine? Behind?

Miz Rain come to the door say, first person. Consuelo go. Then Miz Rain come back say, Next, Jermaine go. Then she call me. We go in little room off side. "This gonna be painless," Miz Rain say, "I just want you to read a page from this little book." All the air go out my body. I grab my stomach. Miz Rain look scared. "Precious!" My head water. I see bad things. I see my daddy. I see TVs I hear rap music I want something to eat I want fuck feeling from Daddy I want die I want die.

"Precious! Are you alright! Breathe! Relax and breathe. Should I call an ambulance? Nine-one-one? Your mother—"

"NO!"

"What's wrong Precious?"

I struggles for air, "I . . . the pages look alike to me." I breave in deep, there I said it.

Miz Rain sigh sad like. "I think I understand you, Precious. But for now, I want you to try, push yourself Precious, go for it."

I reach out my hand for book.

"Just do the best you can, if you don't know a word skip—" She stop. "Just look at the page and say the words you do know."

I look at the page, it's some people at the beach. Some is white, some is orange and gray (I guess thas spozed to be colored).

"What do you think the story is about Precious?"

"Peoples at the beach."

"That's right." Miz Rain point to a letter, ask me what is it. I say, "*A*." She point to some more letters. I don't say nuffin'. "Do you know that word?" No, I don't. "Do you know the letters?" Umm hmmm. She point *D*, then *A*, then *Y*. She say do you know that word? No I don't but I say silence. She say, " 'Day,' that word is 'day.' " She point back at *A*, then "DAY," then point at *A*, *T*, say, "What's that word?" I say, "Ate." She say, "Good! Almost! That word is 'at.' " Then point next word. I say, "The"; then she point last word. I say, "Beach," but I'm not sure, I know *B* in "beach," no *B* in that word. She say, " 'Shore,' that word is 'shore,' that's almost like 'beach,' very good very good," she say. Then she say in soft voice like cat purr (I always wishted I had a cat), "Can you read the whole thing?" I say, "A Day at the Beach." She says very good and closes the book. I want to cry. I want to laugh. I want to hug kiss Miz Rain. She make me feel good. I never readed nuffin' before.

Wednesday can't come fast enuff I'm thinking as I walk down one-two-five. I loves Harlem, especially 125th Street. Lotta stuff out here. You could see we got culchure. I gotta ask my muver for some money for journal book and pay Rhonda back for chips. This gonna be good school for me I know it.

My muver is in the middle of her stories when I come in—TV, TV. She shout on me the minute I open the door.

"Bring your fat ass in here!"

What she think I was doing? I'm tired; I don't want no trouble.

"Where you sneak your ass off to this morning?"

She look like whale on couch. My muver have not left the house in, let's see—1983, '84, '85, '86, 'n now '87. Ever since Little Mongo was born. Social worker come here. I be at school. My grandmuver, Toosie, bring Little Mongo over on days social worker come; game is Little Mongo live here, my mama take care of Little Mongo and me. My mama get check 'n food stamps for me 'n Lil Mongo. But it's *my* baby. Little Mongo is money for me!

"You hear me talking to you! I said where you sneak your ass off to this morning!"

"School!" I shout back. "I was school!"

"You was school?" Mama mimic me how I talk. I hate that! She know what I mean. "You lying whore!"

"Not!"

"You is! The welfare done called here, saying they is removing you from my budget 'cause you not in regular attendance at school."

JeeZUS! Where she been! I told her I got kickted out. I been home three weeks, twenty-four seven. She here when Mrs Lichenstein's white ass come here. I mean Mama what's the deal! Who stupid, me or Mama?

"What you staring at?"

To get to my room I got to walk past Mama. I jus' wanna go to my room.

"I ain' had no breakfast," Mama say.

Oh, so that's it. She want me to cook. Mad 'cause I ain' cook 'fore I left. Shit, get tired of cooking for her. It hard for Mama to stand up long. I look at her. She ain' circus size yet but she getting there. Usta be when I go to regular school Mama make me fix breakfast, bring it to her room 'fore I leave. But since I be outta school I just fix it a little later. She know today I was goin' to alternative.

"I tole you I was goin' to school today."

"Forget school! You better git your ass on down to welfare!"

"I gonna get stipend for school."

"Fool fuck a stipend! What's that. I said take your ass down to welfare NOW!"

"Now?" She know I got to be there at 7 a.m. if I

gonna get to talk to anybody. Welfare very crowded nowadays. "I go in the morning first thing."

Same thing in me when I try to hit Mrs Lichenstein 'n when I grabbed the knife in the dishwater—only deeper. I think my mind a TV set smell like between my muver's legs. I stupid. I ain' got no education even tho' I not miss days of school. I talks funny. The air floats like water wif pictures around me sometime. Sometimes I can't breathe. I'm a good girl. I don't fucks boyz but I'm pregnant. My fahver fuck me. And she know it. She kick me in my head when I'm pregnant. She take *my* money. Money for Little Mongo should be mine. A Day at the Beach Shore A Day A Day ABC Alphabetical order CD ABCD. I grab my notebook. I look at my muver.

"I go to welfare tomorrow—Tuesday. Wednesday I go to school. Monday, Wednesday, and Friday I go to school."

I look Mama. This baby feel like a watermelon between my bones getting bigger and my ankles feelin' tight cause they swoled. I sigh. This gonna end, even if it end by me stop breathing. Thas what I want sometimes. Sometime I hurt so bad I want to not wake up, want breathing to stop in my sleep. Have me *don't* wake up. Other times I start to go a huh a huh ahuh ahuh A HUH A HUH and I grab my chess 'cause I can't breathe, then I *WANT* breathin' bad.

I try to forget I got baby in me. I hated borning the first one. No fun. Hurt. Now again. I think my daddy. He stink, the white shit drip off his dick. Lick it lick it. I

HATE that. But then I feel the hot sauce hot cha cha feeling when he be fucking me. I get so confuse. I HATE him. But my pussy be popping. He say that, "Big Mama your pussy is popping!" I HATE myself when I feel good.

"How long you gonna stand there like you retarded."

I start to tell her don't, don't call me that, but all, everything, is out me. I jus' want to lay down, listen to radio, look at picture of Farrakhan, a *real* man, who don't fuck his daughter, fuck children. Everything feel like it is too big for my mind. Can't nuffin' fit when I think 'bout Daddy.

"I'm tired." Why I say that, she don't care.

"Fix us some lunch, it's way pas' lunch. You done ate?"

"I had some potato chips."

"Thas all?"

I remember ham 'n chicken, don't say nuffin', ax her, "What you want?"

"I don't know, see what's in there. If not nuffin' in there, get stamps out my purse and go to store 'n get us'es somethin' to eat."

ABCDEFGHIJKLMNOPABCDEFGHIJKLMNO PQRS. There are 26 letters in our alphabet. Each letter has a sound. A Day at the Beach Shore ABCDEFGHI JKLMNOPQRSTUVWXYZ.

That night I dream I am not in me but am awake listening to myself choking, going a huh a huh A HUH A HUH A HUH. I am walking around trying to find where I am, where the sound is coming from. I know I will choke to death I don't find myself. I walk to my muver's room but it look different, she look different. I look like little baby almost. She is talkin' sweet to me like sometimes Daddy talks. I am choking between her legs A HUH A HUH. She is smelling big woman smell. She say suck it, lick me Precious. Her hand is like a mountain pushing my head down. I squeeze my eyes shut but choking don't stop, it get worse. Then I open my eyes and look. I look at little Precious and big Mama and feel hit feeling, feel like killing Mama. But I don't, instead I call little Precious and say, Come to Mama but I means me. Come to *me* little Precious. Little Precious look at me, smile, and start to sing: ABCDEFG . . .


Wednesday morning Jo Ann back. She not like G.E.D. I guess. Say she need a little brush up before she go to G.E.D. Miz Rain don't say nuffin' till she hear the brush up stuff, then Miz Rain say, "Are you in the right class Jo Ann? This is a class to learn reading and writing, this is not a brush up for G.E.D." Jo Ann look hate at Miz Rain. I like Miz Rain. I see what she doing, I think. Jo Ann tryin' to act like she ain' one of us. Miz Rain tryin' to git her to 'cept herself for where she at. She ain' no G.E.D. girl, leas' not yet.

Miz Rain call roll: Jermaine Hicks, Rhonda Johnson, Precious Jones, Consuelo Montenegro, Jo Ann Rogers, Rita Romero. Everybody here. Miz Rain ax, "Who wishes to start?" Jo Ann and Jermaine look at her like what she talking. I go to stand up, see Rita Romero done beat me to my feet. She slim, not pretty but she got that light skin that stand for something. Miz Rain look me, say, Gone git up Precious, you can recite together. Rita smile half a smile at me; it's real, but only half 'cause she don't want to show rot teef. I look in her eye, she nod, we go together: ABCDEFGHI JKLMNOPQRSTUVWXYZ.

Then everybody go except Jo Ann. Then Miz Rain ax us to get out our journal books. Mama don't give me no money but I took the change from the food stamps when I was shopping to git one. I got Rhonda's 50 cents too from bottles and cans.

"This is your journal," Miz Rain say. "You're going to write in it everyday." Jo Ann look disgusted, like yeah *right*! One minute we doin' ABCs, next minute we spozed to be writing. Miz Rain give her look like fuck you bitch. I can tell Miz Rain don't like her but she don't say nothin'. She jus' tell us we gonna write in our journals for fifteen minutes everyday.

How, I wonder.

"How," Rhonda say out loud, "*how* we gonna write for fifteen minutes if we can't spell?"

What we gonna write if we could spell, I wonder.

"What," Jermaine throw her two cents in, "what we gonna write?"

Miz Rain say, "Write what's on your mind, push yourself to see the letters that represent the words you're thinking." She turn to me ax real fast, "Precious what's on your mind?" I say, "What?" She say, "What you was thinking just then." I go to open my mouf. She say, "Don't say it, *write* it." I say, "I can't." She say, "Don't say that." She say, "DO what I say, write what you was thinking."

I do:

li Mg o mi m

She tell everyone to not talk and to write for the next fifteen minutes. Everybody is trying something. After time up Miz Rain come to my book ax me to read what I wrote. I reads: "Little Mongo on my mind."

Underneaf what I wrote Miz Rain write what I said in pencil.

li Mg o mi m
*(Little Mongo on my mind)*

Then she write:

Who is Little Mongo?

She read me what she wrote, tell me to *write* my answer to her question in the book. I copy Little Mongo's name from where Miz Rain had wrote it.

Litte mony is mi cie

Miz Rain read, "Little Mongo is my child?" She have question in her voice. I say, "Yes yes." Miz Rain know Little Mongo is my child 'cause I wrote it in my journal. I am happy to be writing. I am happy to be in school. Miz Rain say we gonna write everyday, that mean home too. 'N she gonna write back everyday. Thas great.

I go home. I'm so lonely there. I never notice before. I'm so busy getting beat, cooking, cleaning, pussy and asshole either hurting or popping. School I a joke: black monster, Big Bertha, Blimp B54 where are you? 'N the TV's in my head always static on, flipping picture. So much pain, shame—I never feel the loneliness. It such a small thing compare to your daddy climb on you, your muver kick you, slave you, feel you up. But now since I been going to school I feel lonely. Now since I sit in circle I realize all my life, all my life I been outside of circle. Mama give me orders, Daddy porno talk me, school never did learn me.

It been a month now. I runs in from school nowadays. I don't pretend I'm not pregnant no more. I let it above my neck, in my head. Not that I didn't know it before but now it's like part of me; more than something stuck in me, growing in me, making me bigger. I run past my muver into my room. I wish I had TV in my room. My muver never let me have TV. She say come sit with her. I don't wanna.

I sit in my room. I know too who I'm pregnant for. But I can't change that. Abortion is a sin. I hate bitches who kill they babies. They should kill *them*, see how they like it! I talk to baby. Boy be nice. Girl might be retarded, like me? But I not retarded.

I bet chu one thing, I bet chu my baby can read. Bet a mutherfucker that! Betcha he ain' gonna have no dumb muver.

I look down my stomach. I'm some big now. I'm only seven months but I know I look nine. I mean I am *big*. Scale just stop at 200 but I know if it a different scale like hospital scale it just keep going. I'm going to doctor tomorrow. Miz Rain fall *out*, I mean she fall out! when she finded out I ain' been to doctor. *PRENATAL! PRE-NATAL!* The whole damn class is screamin' *preeeenatal!* Whas that! You gotta this, they say, and you gotta that—I don't gotta though. I don't tell them I had first baby on kitchen floor. Muver kicking me, pains whipping me. Who gonna believe some shit like that?

I look Farrakhan. I look out window at dirt bricks of other building, no sky like school. I got 'nother poster on wall now. Miz Rain give me poster like what we got on wall at school. Thas Harriet nex' to Farrakhan. She leaded over 300 black people out of slavery. You seen *Roots?* I ain't. Miz Rain say see *Roots*, find out what it's all about.

I put my han' on my stomach. I sit here, res' awhile

'fore Mama call me to fix dinner or clean up. It's 26 letters in the alphabet. Each letter got sound. Put sound to letters, mix letters together and get words. You got words. "Baby," start wif *B, b* for "baby," I says in nice soft voice. Soon as he git born I'ma start doing the ABCs. This my baby. My muver took Little Mongo but she ain' taking this one. I am comp'tant. I was comp'tant enough for her husband to fuck. She ain' come in here and say, Carl Kenwood Jones—thas wrong! Git off Precious like that! Can't you see Precious is a beautiful chile like white chile in magazines or on toilet paper wrappers. Precious is a blue-eye skinny chile whose hair is long braids, long long braids. Git off Precious, fool! It time for Precious to go to the gym like Janet Jackson. It time for Precious hair to be braided. Get off my chile nigger!

No, she never say that. Miz Rain say value. Values determine how we live much as money do. I say Miz Rain stupid there. All I can think she don't know to have NOTHIN'. Never breathe and wait for check, check; cry when check late. Check important. Most important. My mama not getting no check for me, I think she be done killed me a long time ago (well maybe not kill me, but thas how I *feel*). Miz Rain say feelin's is important. White woman on the news leave her daddy in desert in a wheelchair when checks run out. He had Alhammer disease. Bitch leave him under a cactus tree wif teddy bear. Don't tell me 'bout check not important.

Mama say this new school ain' shit. Say you can't learn nuffin' writing in no book. Gotta git on that computer you want some money. When they gonna teach you how to do the computer. But Mama wrong. I is learning. I'm gonna start going to Family Literacy class on Tuesdays. Important to read to baby after it's born. Important to have colors hanging from the wall. Listen baby, I puts my hand on my stomach, breathe deep. Listen baby (I writes in my notebook):

A is fr Afrc
  (*for Africa*)
B is for u bae
  (*you baby*)
C is cl w bk
  (*colored we black*)
D is dog
E is el l/m
  (*evil like mama*)
F is Fuck
G is Jerm bt Jer j
  (*Jermaine but Jermaine J*)
ok G is gunn
H hm
  (*home*)
I I somb
  (*somebody*)
J Jer
  (*Jermaine*)
k kl
  (*kill*)

l lv
  (*love*)
M frknka rl m
  (*Farrakhan real man*)
N nf kkk
  (*North America    America=KKK*)
O op
  (*open*)
P ph
  (*punks*)
Q qee litee
  (*Queen Latifah*)
R srt
  (*respect*)
S stp
  (*stop*)
T 2 tn
  (*two ton*)
V vt
  (*vote*)
W wll
  (*well*)
X ma m ml
  (*main man Malcolm*)
Z zk
  (*zonked, mean like high*)

Listen baby, Muver love you. Muver not dumb. Listen baby: ABCDEFGHIJKLMNOPQRSTUVW XYZ.

Thas the alphabet. Twenty-six letters in all. Them letters make up words. Them words everything.

**III**

Boy. It's a boy. Borned at Harlem Hospital January 15, 1988. Abdul Jamal Louis Jones. That is my baby's name. Abdul mean servant of god; Jamal, I forgot; Louis for Farrakhan, of course. At school, new girl Joyce, bring me a book wif African names. I awready had known, Abdul, if it a boy. But I didn't know what it mean.

My name mean somethin' valuable—Precious. Claireece, that somebody else's name. I don't know where my muver get that shit from.

Well, I don't know 'bout baby, I'm happy 'bout baby, I'm sad about baby. Social worker come. I talk to her. She ask 'bout Little Mongo. I tell her Little Mongo wif my grandmother over on St Nicholas Ave. I probably shouldn't have done that. But I was tired. Tired of game, lying. Miz Rain said she read the truth shall set you free; say she not sure she believe it herself. Well, this truth gonna cause Mama to get kicked off welfare. 'Cause what she had been telling the 'fare is Mongo was living with her and she was taking care of bofe of us, so she was getting check for two dependent peoples and stuff. I don't know what's going to happen next. I know I gonna get my own money, but what that if I still in my mama's house? I need my own place, welfare don't give you that much. But main thing above everything else I want to go back to school. Thas all I think about—what they doing? What they reading? Did I miss the feel trip? I think I did.

November was my birthday, I don't tell nobody so don't nobody know. But I light a candle for myself. I glad Precious Jones was born. I like baby I born. It gets to suckes from my bress. First I don't like that. It hurt feel sore, then I like it. He's a good baby. But he's not mine. I mean, he is mine, I push him out my pussy, but I didn't meet a boy 'n fall in love, sex up 'n have a baby.

I think I was rape.

I think what my fahver do is what Farrakhan said the white man did to the black woman. Oh it was terrible and he dood it in front of the black man; that's really terrible. Yeah, on the video, Farrakhan say during slavery times the white man just walk out to the slavery Harlem part where the niggers live separate from the mansions where the white people live and he take any black woman he want and if he feel like it he jus' gone and do the do on top of her even if her man there. This spozed to hurt the black man even more than it hurt the woman getting rape—for the black man to have to see this raping.

My baby is pretty baby. I don't not love him. He is a rapist's baby. But that's OK, Miz Rain say we is a nation of raped children, that the black man in America today is the product of rape.

Still I don't want nobody to know but I tell again like when I was twelve. How can I say baby's fahver unknown when I know?

School, of everything, I know I want to get back to school. I got little baby suckes at my tittie, at my bress. I love Abdul. He normal. But I ain'? I want to go back to school. Abdul in my way. Abdul can not go to Higher Education/Each One Teach One. What I'm gonna do? I love my baby but he ain' mine, he is but I didn't fuck for him. I was raped by my fahver. Now instead of life for me I got Abdul. But I love Abdul. I want go school love abdul schoolabdulschoolabdul.

I write Miz Rain in my journal, when she come hospital she write me back like school:

Dr Miz Ms Rain,
all yr I sit cls I nevr lrn
(*all years I sit in class I never learn*)
bt I gt babe agn Babe bi my favr
(*but I got baby again Babe by my father*)
I wis i had boy_____ but I don
(*I wish I had a boyfriend but I don't*)
ws i had su me fucks a boy lke
(*wish I had excuse me, fucks a boy like*)
or girl den i fel rite dat I have to qk skool
(*other girls then I feel right that I have to quit school*)
i lv baby abcdefghijklmnopqrstuvwxyz
(*I love baby*)

Dear Precious,

Don't forget to put the date, 1/18/88, on your journal entries.

I am glad you love your baby. I think a beautiful young girl like you should get a chance to get an education. I think your first responsibility has to be to yourself. You should not drop out of school. COME BACK TO CLASS. WE MISS YOU.

Love Ms Rain

Ms R    Ja 19, 1988

S_____ wrk as mi i want to gv Litt Mong Abdul up adopsus
(*Social worker ask me if I want to give Little Mongo and Abdul up for adoption*)

I fel ki her
(*I feel kill her*)

Nnevr hep now wnt kiz way
(*Never help now want to take kids away*)

tsak Abdul i don notin
(*take Abdul I don't have nothing*)

Precious,

It seems the opposite to me. If you keep Abdul you might have nothing. You are learning to read and write, that is everything.

Come back to school when you get out the hospital.

You're only seventeen. Your whole life is in front of you.

Ms Rain

1/20

Gr_____ cme vit sa onle dog dro babee an wak off
(*Grandmother come visit say only a dog will drop a baby and walk off*)

say lat no evn a dog
(*say later not even a dog*)

Dear Precious,

Don't forget to put the year, '88, on your journal entries.

Precious you are not a dog. You are a wonderful young woman who is trying to make something of her life. I have some questions for you:

1. Where was your grandmother when your father was abusing you?
2. Where is Little Mongo now?
3. What is going to be the best thing for you in this situation?

Ms Rain

Mss, Rinas
lot qu_____ u ask        Hoo?
(*lot of questions you ask*)   (*Who?*)

Nbi
(*nobody*)
aln
(*alone*)
no Frknm
(*no Farrakhan*)
no mmam
(*no mama*)
no gr____muver fther fucktz me yr
(*no grandmother father fucks me years*)
lii Mongl with my gr____
(*Little Mongo with my grandmother*)
bes four mi tostop breev i sm tim tik
(*best for me to stop breathing I sometimes think*)
aso i want to b god muvther
(*also I wants to be good mother*)

Precious Jones


Dear Dear Precious,

Being a good mother might mean letting your baby be raised by someone who is better able than you to meet the child's needs.

Ms Rain


Mz Rain
Dan frget rite day Ms R
(*Don't forget to write the date Ms Rain.*)
I is be bt meet cldls ed.
(*I is best able to meet my child's need.*)

Ms Precious

Dear Ms Precious, 1/22/88

When you are raising a small infant you need help. Who is going to help you? How will you support yourself? How will you keep learning to read and write?

Ms Rain


Ms Rain
th wfr hlp mma it help mi
(*The welfare help Mama. It help me.*)

Precious Mi


Dear Precious Miss,

When you get home from the hospital look and see how much welfare has helped your mother.

You could go further than your mother. You could get your G.E.D. and go to college. You could do anything Precious but you gotta believe it.

Love Blue Rain


Dear Blu
I lie tah nme Ms Ran. I ty ty
(*I like that name Ms. Rain. I'm tired <u>tired</u>.*)


Well I honestly did wanna jus' take Abdul home 'n rest so I could hurry up 'n go back to school. But when I git home from the hospital Mama try to kill me. I had told myself if she ever come at me like that again I will stab her to def. But when it happen, when she git up off that couch 'n charge toward me like fifty niggers, I ran. I just grab Abdul, my bags, 'n hit the door. I got new baby boy in my arms 'n she calling me bitch hoe slut say she gonna kill me 'cause I ruin her life. Gonna kill me wif her "BARE HANDS!" It's like a black wall gonna crash down on me, nuthin' to do but run. "First you steal my husband! Then you get me cut off welfare!" She MAD! No time to say nothin'. Once I'm outside the door I stop at top of the stairs, look hard at her. She still foaming at mouf, talking about her husband I spoze to steal. I do tell her one thing as I going down the stairs. I say, "Nigger rape me. I not steal shit fat bitch your husband RAPE me RAPE ME!"

I screaming holding little Abdul, hospital bag with Pampers 'n his stuff, 'n a shopping bag from Woolworth's with my stuff in it.

I don't even think, my feets just take me back to Harlem Hospital. You know Koch wanna close it, say niggers don't need no hospital all to theyself. Farrakhan say we need one. Miz Rain say Farrakhan is jive anti-Semitic, homophobe fool. My pussy hurt. I turn down piece of pavement lead to 'mergency. Then I turn back, go through front door, 'n say I wanna visit maternity ward. They not spozed to let you up without hassle 'cause of baby snatchers. But bitch see I got Abdul. She must know if anything I be dropping little homeboy off, not snatching nuffin'.

I get off elevator, looking for Nurse Lenore Harrison, that's Ms Butter's name from when I had Little Mongo. Done worked her way up to queen of the ward. What I gonna be, queen of babies? No, I gonna be queen of those ABCs—readin' 'n writin'. I not gonna stop going to school 'n I not going to give Abdul up and I is gonna get Little Mongo back one day, maybe. I hardly even know what she look like, aside from retarded, that is.

I'm waiting. 'Nother nurse pass me, look at me say she remember me from '83. She skinny, black, I don't remember her. She say she sorry to see me back here, had hoped I be done learned from my mistakes. What kinda shit is that! I didn't make no mistake unless it being born, 'n Miz Rain say I was born for a purpose, 'n Mr Wicher had said I had aptitude for maff. I don't know what purpose but I know I got a purpose, a reason, and according to Farrakhan I got a almighty allah god.

Mistake? I don't think so. Mistakes for niggers to rape. I think I might be the solution. Shit where nurse, yellow bitch. Ize homeless right now. Me 'n Abdul homeless. I can see evil Mama in room tearing posters off wall, messing up my clothes 'n shit. Well bitch gonna hafta get off her ass now!

Nurse Butter come. I tell her what happen. I tell her about school, 'bout Farrakhan 'n allah, 'bout maff—how Mr Wicher had told Mrs Lichenstein I got maff aptitude, and ABCs. How Miz Rain say I'm moving faster through the vowel 'n consonant sounds than even

Rita Romero, who is light skinned. I tell her I not hardly seed Little Mongo since my grandmother tooked her and how Abdul my daddy's baby too. I don't feel shamed—Carl Kenwood Jones freak NOT me!

I am Precious ABCDEFGHIJKLMNOPQRST
  UVWXYZ
My baby is born
My baby is black
I am girl
I am black
I want house to live

Help nurse, help me Miz Lenore. Help me. One thing from going to school 'n talking in class I done learned to talk up. Ms Rain say it's a big country. Say bombs cost more than welfare. Bombs to murder kids 'n shit. Guns to war people—all that cost more than milk 'n Pampers. Say no shame. No shame. Most time it seem like hype, 'cause she say it so much. But that why she say she say it—to reprogram us to love our-selve. I love me. I ain' gonna let that big fat bitch kick my ass 'n shout on me. And I ain' giving Abdul away. And I ain' gonna stop school.

Nurse Butter saying she going off duty now, hate to leave me but got to pick up her daughter from baby-sitter, nurse coming on duty will help me.

I ask new nurse for sanitary napkin, I'm bleeding. This nurse I don't know. She look me kinda cold. She whisper talk some shit to another nurse then come tell me I got to go to the armory. It's like they tired. I'm a problem got to be got out they face. I ain' got no coat, I say. They say people at shelter give me something when I get there. Sit still, van gonna come git me and drop me, and some of the other patients, off. Nurse say lots of people get out hospital wif no place to go, calm down, you not so special.

The armory is like a dungeon of bricks, damp, wif a few 'lectrik lightbulbs hanging from ceiling. A bitch in bed next to bed I'm in hit herself over 'n over in mouf with her own fist. Over 'n OVER. Another girl with swole junkie hands, sores, and shit say, "Put your bags *in* bed with you."

I'm bress feeding Abdul. He cry. He wet. He seem like little rat or cat. I know some things to do for him but I get scared when he cough throw up. He is only seven days old. He could die. Woman, big woman, bigger than me and old—she around forty, come up 'n snatch blanket off my cot. Remind me of Mama, the red light in her eye, the way her hair stick up. What I'm spozed to do; my pussy feel torn apart in pieces, my lower back pain me, my bresses is leaking milk, my bra wet and not smell nice, and maniac done snatched my blanket.

"Give the kid back her blanket," lady wif junkie sores on her arm say.

"Fuck you," maniac say, "I ain' giving back shit."

I jus' take off sheet that's on top the plastic-covered mattress and wrap it around Abdul, then I wrap myself around Abdul and hunker down on that cold plastic. I wish they would turn the lights out. But they don't. I go to sleep anyway. When I wake up bags with my stuff gone, one of my shoes the laces is untied. Maybe that's what wake me up, them trying to get the shoes off my feet. How many days I lay up in Mama's house thinking nothing could be worse than that. I get up, tie my shoes. These bitches here crazy. I feed Abdul. My body is his breakfast. I gotta get something to eat myself.

I'm at armory not far from hospital. This shit ain' gonna work. What time is it? Six a.m. Miz West! Live down the hall from us, stop Mama from kicking me to death when Mongo being born. She like me. I always did go to the store for her since I was little.

"Precious, bring me back a pack of Winstons and a big bag of pork rinds."

"Yes Miz West."

"Keep the change Precious."

One time she tell me, You ever wanna talk about anything you could come to me.

But I never did. And I don't know her phone number now. How would she get in Mama's house to get my stuff out anyway?

"Breakfast?" dope addict girl say.

"Yeah," I say. Lots of the girlz, womens, is moving toward a door. Some just sit on the bed cots like they in shock or some shit. Dope addict girl point at people moving, say follow them. I do.

Coffee out a steel pitcher, a little box of cornflakes, and a banana. I don't drink coffee. It's almost 7 o'clock.

Fuck it, I go wait for Ms Rain in lobby. Maybe it be one of those days she come in early. I wait there till 8:45 a.m. She is shock when she walk through door and see me sitting on floor of lobby in Hotel Theresa wif Abdul in my arms. I almost forgit about me for a minute, I feel so sorry for her. She just ABC teacher, not no social worker or shit. But where else can I go?

I can tell by Ms Rain's face I'm not gonna be homeless no more. She mumbling cursing about *what* damn safety net, most basic needs, a newborn child, *A NEW-BORN CHILD!* She going OFF now. Rhonda come in behind her. No class, all of Each One Teach One is on the phone! They calling everybody from Mama to the mayor's office to TV stations! Before this day is up, Ms Rain say, you gonna be living somewhere, as god is my witness. As GOD is my witness!

Thas when Queens shit come up. They wanna send me to ½way house in Queens, immediate opening! NO! What I know about Queens?! They got Arabs, Koreans, Jews, and Jamaicans—all kinda shit me and Abdul don't need to be bothered with. Here, I stay here in Harlem. Harlem house say they couldn't take me for two weeks. Ms Rain's boss git on phone. She is West Indian woman, don't take no shit. Boyfriend sit on some council. She hang up phone, say, They can take her tomorrow. So they just have to find me a place for tonight. Everyone says I can stay over their house. But you know where I stay? Ms Rain got friend who is caretaker or something at Langston Hughes' house which is not but around the corner, it's city landmark. I SPEND ONE NIGHT IN LANGSTON HUGHES' HOUSE HE USED TO LIVE IN. Me and Abdul in the Dream Keeper's house! Day after that, we come here, where I been ever since. Here, at Advancement House, main good thing is they got somebody we can trust to take care of our babies while we go to school for four hours a day, three times a week. Queens, no Ms Rain, no school.

I like my room here. Better than home, Mama's house, I mean. I got bed for me, crib for Abdul. Dresser drawers, desk, chair, bookcase for my books and Abdul's books. Some of my books is:

1. *The Life of Lucy Fern* 1 and 2 (it's two books) by Moira Crane
2. *Pat King's Family* by Karen McFall
3. *Harriet Tubman: Conductor on the Underground Railroad* by Ann Petry
4. *Wanted Dead or Alive: The True Story of Harriet Tubman* by Ann McGovern (got *two* Harriet books!)
5. *Malcolm X* by Arnold Adoff
6. *A Piece of Mine* by J. California Cooper
7. *The Color Purple* by Alice Walker
8. *Selected Poems* by Langston Hughes

some books Abdul got:

1. *The Black BC's* by Lucille Clifton
2. *Harold and the Purple Crayon* by Crockett Johnson

3. *The Story of a Little Mouse Trapped in a Book*
   by Monique Felix
4. *The Boy Who Didn't Believe in Spring* by
   Lucille Clifton
5. *Hi, Cat!* by Ezra Jack Keats

Most of what we got Ms Rain give us. I would like a job, a paycheck—be able to buy what I want when I want it.

We reading *The Color Purple* in school. Which is really hard for me. Ms Rain try to break it down but most of it I can't read myself. But the rest of the class kinda can, 'cept Rita. But how Ms Rain hook it up I am getting something out the story. I cry cry *cry* you hear me, it sound in a way so much like myself except I ain' no butch like Celie. But just when I go to break on that shit, go to tell class what Five Percenters 'n Farrakhan got to say about butches, Ms Rain tell me I don't like homosexuals she guess I don't like her 'cause she one. I was shocked as shit. Then I jus' shut up. Too bad about Farrakhan. I still believe allah and stuff. I guess I still believe everything. Ms Rain say homos not who rape me, not homos who let me sit up not learn for sixteen years, not homos who sell crack fuck Harlem. It's true. Ms Rain the one who put the chalk in my hand, make me queen of the ABCs.

Oh, I not tell you that! Every year mayor's office give awards to outstanding students in literacy pro-

grams. Well, this year, 1988, it was me. After I get in
½way house (which turn out to be only ½way cool 'cause
some of the bitches there is Sick with a capital $S$ (capital letter is how you start off sentence or say something
with deep shit meaning like Fuck with capital $F$ you
mad or some shit like that!). But like I said the good
thing, the real good thing, about ½way house is it in
Harlem so I could keep going to school easy.

So anyway by February I'm pretty settled in
Advancement House. So I work all spring, memorizing
letter sounds, writing in journal, reading books. I have
read *Pat King's Family* 'bout white woman whose husband abuse 'n abandon her. I have read *Ain Nobodi Gon'
Turn Me 'Round* 'bout civil rights. I ain' know black people in this country went through shit like that. But thas
the deal here in cracker jack city as Farrakhan say. So
anyway I made so much progress I won award. Literacy
Award. I get it September of 1988. Ms Rain wanted to
give it to me even before then. She say she had wanted
to give it to me after I come back from Abdul being
born and homeless 'n stuff. But director say, Well, we
got other students who deserve it, let's see if Precious
got staying power.

So I get award from mayor's office, money ($75) from
Each One Teach One, and class have a party for me.

Things going good in my life, almost like *The Color
Purple*. Abdul nine months old, *walking*! Smart smart.
He smart. I been reading to him since day he was born
damn near. I love *The Color Purple*, that book give me so

much strength. Ms· Rain say a group of black men wanted to stop movie from the book. Say unfair picture of nigger men. She ax me what do *I* think. Unfair picture? Unfortunately it a picture I know, except of course Farrakhan who is real man. But I never seen him 'cept on videos! He say problem is not crack but the cracker! I go for that shit.

Ms Rain say one of the critcizsm of *The Color Purple* is it have fairy tale ending. I would say, well shit like that can be true. Life can work out for the best sometimes. Ms Rain love *Color Purple* too but say realism has its virtues too. Izm, smizm! Sometimes I wanna tell Ms Rain shut up with all the IZM stuff. But she my teacher so I don't tell her shut up. I don't know what "realism" mean but I do know what REALITY is and it's a mutherfucker, lemme tell you.

Mama come to ½way house. (What is ½way house? I thought I already told you. But anyway I tell you from book I read about battered woman. In a way I was a battered woman but I was not a woman—actually I was a chile. And it wasn't my husband. I don't have a husband. It was my muver.) But anyway, I never reading no book about a place for children, jus' for grown-up women (in a way I am that too) and babies. But this book I was reading was about a woman who got beat up by her husband. And she escape to ½way house. She asks people at the place just what ½way house is. They tell her, You is ½way between the life you had and the life you want to have. Ain't that nice. You should read that book if you have a chance.

So I'm in ½way house, I been there, oh, not quite a year; like in book I read—I'm on threshold of stepping out into my new life, an apartment for me, Abdul, and maybe Little Mongo, we see on that one, mo' education, new friends. I done left Mama, Daddy, Ms Lichenstein, I.S. 146 behind. So I'm wondering what hoe want wif me. Can't get no money. I went see about Little Mongo back when I first get in Advancement House. They put her in institution, say she severely (mean real) retarded, and Toosie hadn't been doing things that would help her—like colors on the wall and books 'n shit, so she really in bad shape. They say even if she could be help, take a lot more than me to help, and ain't I got full load with Abdul.

Anyway live-in social worker at Advancement House call me into office, say, Precious, your mother is here to see you. Ax me do I want to see her. I say OK. (It's not like I *want* to see her but since she comed all this way here I will see her. She know better, I think, than to fuck wif me now.)

I walk in dayroom. Mama quiet. Mama look bad, don't have to get close to know she smell bad. But then I look Mama and see my face, my body, my color—we bofe big, dark. Am I ugly? Is Mama ugly? I'm not sure. I know she got pussy odor and ugly brogan shoes like people make fun of and giant green dress that her legs come out of like black jelly elephant legs. I'm ashamed, this is my Mama. No matter how fly my braids is, how I grease my skin, scalp, no matter how many jew'ries, this is my mother.

Mama don't look me in eye. She never did 'less she was shouting on me or telling me what to do—cook her something or go to store. She look down say, "Your daddy dead." She come out the house to tell me that! So what! I'm glad the nigger's dead. No, I don't mean that, but so what. Mama quiet. Mama say, "Carl had the AIDS virus."

You know, so what, why you telling me. Then oh! No! Oh no, I get all squozen inside. Carl fuckes me. I could be done have it. Abdul could be—oh no, I can't even say nuffin'.

A long time I don't say nuffin', jus' look at Mama. This what I come out of? Like Abdul and Little Mongo come out of me. If she ever said a kind word to me I don't remember it. Sixteen years I live in her house without knowing how to read. Since I was little her husband fuck me beat me. My daddy. I want to hate him—but it's funny I, he, give me the only good thing in my life aside from Ms Rain, ABCs, and girls at school; Abdul come from him, my son, my brother. But Mama give me to him. This my mother. Carl come in the night, take food, what money they is, fuck us bofe. Something cross my mind now. Man rape Celie turn out not to be her daddy.

"Mama?"

She look over where I'm at.

"Yo' huzbn, Carl, my real daddy?" I ask.

"What chu mean?"

"Carl, was he my real daddy? Was you married to him for real?"

"He your daddy, couldn't no one else be your daddy. I was with him since since I was sixteen. I never been with nobody else. We not married though, he got a wife though, a real wife, purty light-skin woman he got two kids by."

Hmmm, they got special kinda AIDS for yellow bitches? Mama! Thought jus' now hit me, don't know why, it the most obvious—do Mama got it?

"You got it?" I ask.

"No."

"How you know?"

"We never did, you know—"

I look at Mama like she fucking crazy! What she talking about?

"You know," she repeat. "What you got to do to get it."

"He never fuck you," I say shock.

"Oh yeah," she say. "But not like faggots, in the ass and all, so I know—"

Her voice trail off, stupid bitch. I'm jus' staring at her. I wanna kill her. I remember what I know from AIDS Awareness Day at school. Look at Mama, say, "You better get tested."

That's all really I got to say. Mama look at me like she wanna say something.

"You welcome back home," she say.

"I home here," I say. Silence. "Well I guess I better go see 'bout Abdul 'n do homework." Mama don't move. So, you know, I jus' get up and leave.

Song playing in my head now, not rap. Not TV colors flashing funny noise pictures in on me, scratching and itching in my brain at the same time. I see a color I don't know the name for, maybe one like only another kind of animal thas not human can see. Like butterflies? I ask Ms Rain tomorrow do butterflies see colors. Song caught on me like how plastic bags on tree branches. I sit on my bed. New picture on wall now. I got Alice Walker up there with Harriet Tubman 'n Farrakhan. But she can't help me now. Where my *Color Purple*? Where my god most high? Where my king? Where my black love? Where my man love? Woman love? Any kinda love? Why me? I don't deserve this. I not crack addict. Why I get Mama for a mama? Why I not born a light-skin dream? Why? Why? It's a movie, splashing like swimming pool at Y, in my head. I see Abdul running away from me, he is like little animal running toward a cliff, I am running running too, all over is clowns with evil eyes laffing at me I can't run fast enuff, the music is playing louder now I going off cliff myself now, maybe I don't come back. Don't see Abdul. A huh! A Huh! I can't breathe! Song loud now real loud. I stop running. It's grass green all aroun'. I listen to song, I can hear it now. It's Aretha. I always did wish she was my mother or Miss Rain or Tina Turner; a mother I be proud of, love me. I breathe in, lay down on my bed. Bed, I remember, I finded for myself when Mama go off on me that last time. Aretha singing, "Gotta find me an angel gotta find me an angel in my liifffe."

Heart hurt. I don't know what to do. If not for Abdul (name mean servant of god) I . . . I . . . my god, Jezus— allah most high, ABDUL! Mama, Carl, me, Abdul Abdul Abdul, he my angel, my little angel. Do Abdul got it?

I don't know what to do. I ask Ms Rain tomorrow.

On the wall under pictures of Harriet, Alice Walker, and Farrakhan is my Literacy Award. That is good proof to me I can do anything. Already Abdul know ABC. Plus he know his numbers. Barely talk and he counting. I did that. One day I going back for Little Mongo. Maybe I make the day sooner than I had thought. Time, I want to learn to look at round clock and tell time. No one ever show me. I never tell Ms Rain I don't know that. Got everything like digital watch display, them watches from Korea. What's the difference between Korean and Jap? Mr Wicher say I got aptitude for maff. Where I gonna go when I leave ½way house? I got AIDS? HIV? What's the difference? My son got it? Lil Mongo? How I gonna learn and be smart if I got the virus? Why me? Why me? Maybe virus don't get me? Maybe, I, jus' 'cause Carl have it don't mean me and Abdul have it.

I gotta go upstairs to the nursery to get Abdul. I think about this later. It make me feel stupid crazy, I mean stupid crazy.

I don't say nuffin' Monday in school, Ms Rain ax me what wrong. I say, I OK, talk about it later. Ms Rain say what about now. I write her in my journal book.

Jan 9, 1989

One yr I ben scool I like scool I love my techr
(*One year I been school I like school I love my teacher*)
lot i lern. Books I read, chile care work comprts
(*lot I learn. Books I read, child care, work computers*)
Ms Rain i wood like to get a gud job lern wrk comptrs
(*Ms Rain I would like to get a good job learn work computers*)
get apt me n lil Mongo and Abdul
(*get apartment me and Little Mongo and Abdul*)
Ms Rain I ass you wy Me?
(*Ms Rain I ask you why Me?*)

Precious

Dear Ms Precious,

You make my day! You don't just don't know how much I love having you in class, how much I love you period. And I am proud of you; the whole school is proud of you.

I'm sure you'll be able to find a job when you get your G.E.D. And maybe your social worker could help you get a nice place for you, Little Mongo, and Abdul.

I don't know what you mean by your question, "Why me?" Please explain.

Ms Rain 1/9/89

Blue,
So many time u say i cood call you bi yr firs name. I nver doo.
(*So many time you say I could call you by your first name. I never do.*)

> Blu Ran
> Blue RAIN
> Rain
> is gr____
>    (*gray*)
> but saty
>       (*stay*)
> my rain

A pome
(*a poem*)
that all i hav to say rit now

1/11/89<br>Precious Jones<br>the poet

1/13/89

I talk to s_____ wrk tody she gonn get tess for me
(*I talk to social worker today she gonna get test for me*)

an Abdul (se_____ of God) to see
(*and Abdul (servant of God) to see*)

see the i

ey see
(*eye*)

see me

liv
(*live*)

or

die

poslv
(*positive*)

or

negv
(*negative*)

wh? wh?
(*why? why?*)

must

I li
(*lie*)

to misel
(*myself*)

I

must

P U S H

no
(*know*)
the truf
(*truth*)

Precious P. Jones

1/13/89
Dear Precious POET Jones!
   Awesome! I love your poetry and your draw-
ings. What are you and Abdul going to see?
   How did you like the poems we read in class?
Love Ms Blue Rain

Ms Rain
Mi an Abdul got a scrit
(*Me and Abdul got a secret*)
I tell yo latr promois
(*I tell you later promise*)
no i tell yo now
IV HIV HIV U an Mi coold hav HIV
(*IV HIV HIV You and me could have HIV*)
mi sun God Allh
(*my son God Allah*)
Alice Walk pra o IV VI YWXYZ
(*Alice Walker pray oh IV VI YWXYZ*)
I ah V I I H IH I HIV
HIV.

Precious P. Jones

Dear Precious,                              1/23/89

　　Are you saying you and Abdul need to take
an HIV test? Well, tell me as much as you feel
comfortable.

Ms Rain

Blue wmon

who tech mi who hep mi I don no whut
(*who teach me who help me I don't know what*)

to sa it hard to xplxn i nver tel mi hole store. Yes I
(*to say it hard to explain I never tell my whole story. Yes I*)

need tess four AID I skred thas ALL four nov
(*need test for AIDS. I scared that's ALL for now*)

pane
(*pain*)

Precious Pane
(*Pain*)

2/1/89

I gotta learn more than ABCs now. I got to learn more
than read write, this big BIG. This the biggest thing
happen to Precious P. Jones in her life. I got the AIDS
virus. Thas what tess say. We sitting in circle thas
when I tell class. Jus' like it's cornflakes for breakfast.
After so many days looking out the window, doing
double talk in my journal. I just come out and say it.

　　"Nurse at clinic say to me, You are HIV positive," I

say to girls, we sit in circle, some faces new, some the same faces from first day—Rita Romero, she hanged. Jermaine still here, Consuelo gone. Rhonda still on set, some new girls—who is like me when I first walk through the door. Only now I the one who say "keep on keepin' on!" to new girls. I show them how the dialogue journal work. You know how you write to teacher 'n she write back to you in the same journal book like you talkin' on paper and you could SEE your talk coming back to you when the teacher answer you back. I mean thas what had made me really like writing in the beginning, knowing my teacher gonna write me back when I talk to her. I explain the phonics game, vocab building list—all stuff like that *I* know now. We have a class project—LIFE STORY. It's where we write our life stories and put it all in one big book. From the girls who been here awhile I only one ain' done my story yet. One day when I have time I read you what the other girls wrote. Some bitches get down, some bullshit. When I hear Rhonda's story, Rita Romero's story, I know I not the worse off. Rita's daddy kill her mother in front her eyes. Rita been on street selling pussy since she was twelve. She the only one came in like me—can't read, write nothin'. Then Rhonda's brother raping her since she was a chile, her mother fine out and put Rhonda, not brother, out. Consuelo in fantasy land, she pretty, long hair. But I glad she gone. She wave her pretty in my face like a flag, tell me exercise and stay out sun so I don't get no darker. Say she found good man.

I glad. I don't hate no one. I don't hate Mama, Carl, so why I gonna get bent outta shape behind some Spanish talking bitch who bent outta shape 'cause she dark like nigger instead of white. Shit, Rhonda a nigger and she lighter than Consuelo! Consuelo did leave but Jermaine didn't follow behin' her. Jermaine stayed on. She write real in book. Call what she is sexual preference. Say she shouldn't be judge 'cause of that. She got hard rock story too. Say mens beat her for what she is. Mother put her out house when she fine out.

These girlz is my friends. I been like the baby in a way 'cause I was only 16 first day I walk in. They visit at hospital when I had Abdul and take up a collection when Mama kick me out and bring stuff to ½way house for me—clothes, cassette player, tuna fish, and Cambull soup, and stuff. They and Ms Rain is my friends and family.

Ms Rain a butch. This still shock to me 'cause you can not tell it, but I remember what she said—not homos who rape me, not homos who let me be ignerent. I forgets all that ol' shit lately—Five Percenters, Black Israelites, etc etc (etc etc mean yeah yeah). I never be butch like Celie but it don't make me happy—make me sad. Maybe I never find no love, nobody. At least when I look at the girls I see *them* and when they look they see *ME*, not what I looks like. But it seems like boyz just see what you looks like. A boy come out my pussy. Was nothing. A dark spot in the sky; then turn to life in me. When he grow up he gonna laff big black girls? He gon' laff at dark skin like he got? One thing I say about Farrakhan and Alice Walker they help me like being black. I wish I wasn't fat but I am. Maybe one day I like that too, who knows.

But I look my friends in the circle and I tell them, test say I'm HIV positive. And all the tongues dead, can't talk no more. Rita Romero hug me like I'm her chile and I cry and Ms Rain rub my back and say let it out, Precious, let it out. I cry for every day of my life. I cry for Mama what kinda story Mama got to do me like she do? And I cry for my son, the song in my life. The little brown penis, booty, fat thighs, roun' eyes, the voice of love say, Mama, Mama he call me.

Then crying stop. Rita go to her purse and get magazine call *Body Positive* say I got to join HIV community. Jezus! It's a community of them? Us, I mean. But I tell her, Not now. I just need to think. Is life a hammer to beat me down? Jermaine jump up do boxing dance (she think she Mike Tyson!) say fight back! I laugh, a little.

Ms Rain say we got to write now in our journals. Say each of our lives is important. She got us book from Audre Lorde, a writer woman like Alice Walker. Say each of us has a story to tell. What is a black unicorn? I don't really understand the poem but I like it.

I don't have nothing to write today—maybe never. Hammer in my heart now, beating me, I feel like my blood a giant river swell up inside me and I'm drowning. My head all dark inside. Feel like giant river I never cross in front me now. Ms Rain say, You not writing

Precious. I say I drownin' in river. She don't look me like I'm crazy but say, If you just sit there the river gonna rise up drown you! Writing could be the boat carry you to the other side. One time in your journal you told me you had never really told your story. I think telling your story git you over that river Precious.

I still don't move. She say, "Write." I tell her, "I am tired. Fuck you!" I scream, "You don't know nuffin' what I been through!" I scream at Ms Rain. I never do that before. Class look shock. I feel embarrass, stupid; sit down, I'm made a fool of myself on top of everything else. "Open your notebook Precious." "I'm tired," I says. She says, "I know you are but you can't stop now Precious, you gotta push." And I do.

# IV

2/27/89

Ms Rain say more now, much more. She wan
more from me. More than 15 minutes an she
write back. Say walk wif it. The *journal?* I say.
Yeah, she say, Walk wif da journl. Everywhere
you go, ~~journl~~ journal go. You know I go walk
with Abdul etc., take journal, write stuff in
journal.

learnin lot: to too two. three diffrent 2 words.
Each one is ~~diffrent~~ different. Four for fore.
Three four words.

Stori

Ms Rain tell me to <u>k</u>oncentrate on my story.
When I ~~ka~~ can not spell a word Ms Rain tell me
sound out firs lettr c____ and draw a lin. Thas
concentrate. Latrer she will fill in rite spelling
for me.

But my spelling is impruv. Way way improve.

Ms Rain say I seem dpress
deprs<u>sion</u> is she say angr<u>er</u> turn in.

Jermaine say not n<u>ecessarily</u> rally
(Whutevr Ms Rain say Jermaine don agree)


Rite wRite write
more she say
talk more
    say ~~gte~~ get ½ hos staf to get babee sitter xtra
hr so I can go to meatings, movie.
    You no I never (good spell) bin a movie, cep
vidios on Mama's VCR. I never bin chuc. Rhonda
goe ALL the time. Want take me an Ms Rain.
She want take hole skool sins she bin savd.


For
a monf it bin like this. I feel daze.
Ms Rain see it
    say you not same girl i kno.
    is tru. I am a difrent
    persn
    anybuddy wood be don't u think?
    dont
    u
    think.


Ms Rain
    say go back back back
    far
    you

can rember.
what four? I say
whut i got to rmember i nevr dun forgit
mama daddy scool
Y why go thru ALL (i like that word) DAT
ALL DAT
ALL DAT
SHIT
But Ms Rain
worred worryed worried about mi.
Thas nice sumebuddy care but I don want to
worri her. She sen note ½way hous for me to cum
scool ½ hr erly to write. And go downtown wif
Rhonda for insect talk grup and chuc. I think I
AM
MAD.
ANGERREEY          angerry
very
mi life
not good
i got dizeez. Ms Rain
say NOT dizeez
I say whut is it then.
I Talk
angr
to Ms Rain
she say u notice yr spelin change wen yu hav
feelins not tal bout in book she say i am nt dyslx
nune that say its emoshunal disturb lets talk bout it

I was fine til HIV thing
she say i still fine
but prblm not jus HIV it mama Dady
BUT I was gon dem
I escap dem like Harriet
Ms Ran say we can nt escap the pass.
the way free is hard
look Harriet H-A-R-R-I-E-T
i pratise her name.
Rita say keep tinkin whut you got to bee
thankfill for
Jermaine (she bes writer in skool) say semicoln
no coln
go befour list
:
i gt two bee thankfill four:
Ms Rain
~~seool~~ school
girlz in class
Abdul
Toosday Rita take me VILLAG
Sat we go muzeum

sun day chuch
MONDY we gonna read Harriet T. book

I feel btretter 🙂 glad I write my book

Precious

3/6/89

Wat it be like to bee in luv. I wondr this al the time ALL time all the time.

I kno sex sex so much. I kno bout sex alot a lot wht it be like to hav a fren, thas a guy I mean.

I GOT frens.

I don't sho Ms Rain everything in my book no mor. she mi techer Don want her kno if I rite about SEX if I have sex wif a kute coot boy thas my own age I wil _____.

Rita got a man. Rhonda God. Ms Rain a fren. Jermaine say hole worl her lovr.


3/8/89

My favrt thing to take Abdul down to nursery at
breakfus
then
not eat breakfus. n that giv me time
to
wallk throo Harlem in
mornin to school
mostly pepul goin
to work
faces faces
iron brown
black glas
tears
not jazzee
Harlem

of Langston Huges
Harlmen Poet Laureeyet!
this
a Harlem done
took
a beating
but
mornin
if you
like
me
you see
ILANATHA tree rape
concreet
n birf
spiky green
trunk
life.
see
mens in
vaykent lot bild
fire
lik indiens
shar
whut
they got.
Bus
roll
mostlee wmen

PUSH

downtwn
sky opn
blu legs
for
sun.


   I hit 116th n sometimes I walk up Madison
and go aroun the park, the park nevr clean but
green. Pas bafhouse. Bafhouse where faggits meet
nekkid fuck each other. I wondr wat that be like.
trees. after park liberry on 124th. I got libry card.
Nex door libry is none house. Nones live ther
serve god don fuck. Rhonda say you go in base-
ment where nones live is babee bones. Rita say
das a lie. She Kathlic. I say God. Sho me god.
Keep going down 124th vaykent lot.


        i stop. Gon rite bout vaykent lot.
        uuuuuuugh dog shit dog shit
           crummel up briks
           steell fence
           lifes of trash
           cancer yr eye
           multiply
           ugliness
           greazee shit
           garbage cans, rottin
           cloze PAMPER filthee

dope addicks
pile up
flow ovr
uglee
I HATE
HATE
UGLY

turn from vaykent lot n is vaykent pepul with
kraters like what u see wen you look at spots on
the moon. wen you see moon on space movies is
holes on it, kraters. thas on dope addicts arms—
kraters. Dese not crack addicts like on one-two-
six. Dese people on 1-2-4 is HAIRRUN shuters.
There eyez is like far away space ships. they don
see you, only smell pepul go buy for money.
They money dogs. If they sniff money they will
try to take it. I guess. Thas whut I always here. I
nevr reely had a dope addict hurt me. We hate
dope addicts. We, me, norml pepul. I git confuse
how i git wif dope addicts. How whut they got I
got. I don unnerstan DOPE. Whut I see do not
look like fun. it look SAD. It look teef fall out.
they have gums not teef, talk funny, walk stupid.
WHY? If I stay on 124th to 7th Ave more
vaykent lot. Maybee pass nigger wif needle in
his arm noddin in the wind. Drops of blood
drip down. maybe pass sex sicko wif peniss out,

flashlite eyes shine sperms on you. Its a block like a fog wif worms. the pepul worms. I hate em. UGLY.

But confuse.

Across from bar on Lenox btween 124 n 125 is only zerox shop in Harlm. blak sister and dater own it. when zerox at school break down I cum there git zerox. in shop she got books, cards, blak stuff I hardley ever have money to buy stuff. I DIE for I steel. Nver will Precious Jones steel (no more) or shute dope.

Thas whut tv sho, niggers steel shute dope steel shute dope harlm crime crime. On top bar is Diane McIntyre's skool. I wood hav liked to go to dancin scool when I was young. Its too late now. I'm eighteen. An Abdul a boy. Boyz don go Only faggit boyz. I don want Abdul to be faggit or dope addick.

But what I confuse about is this. Itz so uglee dope addicks—dey teef, dey underwater walkin, steelin. Spred AIDS an heptietis.

But Rita was one of dese pepul an she is GOOD. I luv her.


When I get to school early sometimes I just sit in front part on the black plastic couch that need tape where it cut and the yellow foam pads show through. School start at 9 o'clock. The secretary get here at 8:00 a.m. I don' get here before that 'cause the door locked and I would have to wait in the lobby downstairs. Which I don't like.

Our room is nice. Nicer since we have one day where we come in "raggedy" and bring our own cleaning stuff 'n posters, pictures, 'n plants from home 'n fix up our room. Ms Rain say bring something of YOU! I bring picture of Abdul and plant from Woolworth on 125th Street. It growed. Leaves big. Ms Rain done changed its pot three times.

Ms Rain get here 'bout 8:15 or so, usually right behind or in front of Rita or Rhonda. They bofe erly birds too. Ms Rain jus' give whoever here the keys from her purse to open up our classroom while she do whatever she do—fix coffee, git books from supply room—stuff like that. By 8:30 a.m. early birds good to go! Room quiet sunny. We just open our notebook, Ms Rain usually say something like, You got 10 or 15 minutes 'fore the "rabble" get here. Yeah, I don't know exactly what is the rabble. She jus' joking for Jermaine and them who hit the door roun' 9:05 a.m. Always a little late, always complaining 'bout something—the weather, train, what the newspaper say.

Me, I, just look at the sun coming in through the front window. Pretty soon it move around and come in through the side window. I like the routine of school, the dream of school. I wonder where I be if I had been learning all those years I sit at I.S. 146. Favorite book?

Maybe it's our book, the big book with all our stories in it. Not mine yet. I'm just putting stuff in my journal now.

Telling time is *easy*. Fractions, percents, multiplying, dividing is EASY. Why no one never taught me these things before. Rita say, All people with HIV or AIDS is innocent victims; it's a disease, not a "good," a "bad." You know what she mean? Well, thas good 'cause I don't. I cannot see how I am the same as a white faggit or crack addict. Rita kiss my forehead, hold each my cheeks with her hands, look me in my eyes, "Negra," she say, her eyes big like babies', black black eyes. "You don't see now but will. You will."

I don't know how I will, I don't even know what she's talkin' about. She's talking about *Life*, Ms Rain say. Well, I don't know what life is all about either. I know I'm eighteen, magic number. And my reading score is 2.8. I ask Ms Rain what that mean. She say it's a number! And can't no numbers measure how far I done come in jus' two years. She say forget about the numbers and just keep working. The author has a message and the reader's job is to decode that message as thoroughly as possible. A good reader is like a detective, she say, looking for clues in the text. A good reader is like you Precious, she say. Passionate! Passionately involved with whut they are reading. Don't worry about numbers and fill in the blank, just read and write!

I'm changing. Things I don't care about no more:

if boyz love me
extensions
new clozes

what I care about is:

STAYING HEALTHY
sex (____)
notebook, writing poems

Ms Rain say don't always rhyme, stretch for words to fall like drops of rain, snowflakes—did you know no two snowflakes is alike? Have you ever seen a snowflake? I haven't! All I seen is gobs of dirty gray shit. You mean to tell me that nasty stuff is made of snowy flakes. I don't believe it.

Each day is different. All the days is gobbed together to make a year, all the years gobbed together to make a life. I have a secret. Secret is, I mean I think Rita and Ms Rain halfway know but they too nice to get any further in my business than I want them in. I mean I have kids. But I never have a guy, you know like that. It never usta be on my mind. All I want before is Daddy get the fuck off me! But now I think about *that*, you know, that being fucking a cute boy. I think about that and I think about being a poet or rapper or an artist even. It's this guy on one-two-five, Franco, he done painted pictures on the steel gates that's over almos' all the store windows. At night you walk down and each one is painted different. I like that better than museum.

It's so many different ways to walk the few blocks home. Turn a corner and you see all different. Pass 116th 'n Lenox, more abandoned land, buildings falling down. How it git so ugly is people throw trash all in it. City don't pick it up; dogs doo doo. Peoples wif no bafroom piss 'n shit. Ugliness grow multiplied by ten. Keep walkin' down Lenox to one-twelve you pass projects. I never did live in projects. I live in 444 Lenox Avenue almost all my life. Where I live before that house I don't know, maybe wif my grandmother.

Wonder about Mama sometimes. Wonder about Carl more. Carl Kenwood Jones. I got session wif counselor today. Last week we try to figure out how long I been infected. People at retard place say Lil Mongo don't got it. She say that could mean Daddy get AIDS pretty fast from time he first infected to time he die? 'Cause if Lil Mongo don't got it maybe he didn't have it 1983 when she born. Then after she born he go away a long time. So maybe I get it eighty-six, eighty-seven? Counselor say, I'm on top now. I'm young, is got no disease and stuff, not no drug addict. I could live a long time, she say. I ask her what's a long time. She don't say.

I think some of the girls at Advancement House know I am . . . am *positive*. I mean wifout trying I know some of they bizness. They never was too friendly; since Mama come wif her news, they even less friendly. But who cares? I'm not tight wif these girls in the house. These bitches got problems, come in room and steal shit. I know I ain' the only one that got it, even though that's how it feels. But I'm probably the only one get it from they daddy. Counselor, Ms Weiss, say she try to find out as much about Daddy for me as she can.

How much I want to know? And for what? I tell counselor I can't talk about Daddy now. My clit swell up I think Daddy. Daddy sick me, *disgust* me, but still he sex me up. I nawshus in my stomach but hot tight in my twat and I think I want it back, the smell of the bed-room, the hurt—he slap my face till it sting and my ears sing separate songs from each other, call me names, pump my pussy in out in out in out awww I come. He bite me *hard*. A hump! He slam his hips into me HARD. I scream pain he come. He slap my thighs like cowboys do horses on TV. Shiver. Orgasm in me, his body shak-ing, grab me, call me Fat Mama, Big Hole! You LOVE it! Say you love it! I wanna say I DON'T. I wanna say I'm a chile. But my pussy popping like grease in frying pan. He slam in me again. His dick soft. He start suck-ing my tittie.

I wait for him get off me. Lay there stare at wall till wall is a movie, *Wizard of Oz*, I can make that one play anytime. Michael Jackson, scarecrow. Then my body take me over again, like shocks after earthquake, shiver me, I come again. My body not mine, I hate it coming.

Afterward I go bafroom. I smear shit on my face. Feel good. Don't know why but it do. I never tell nobody about that before. But I would do that. If I go to insect support group what will I hear from other girls. I bite my fingernails till they look like disease, pull strips of my skin away. Get Daddy's razor out cabinet. Cut cut cut arm wrist, not trying to die, trying to plug myself back in. I am a TV set wif no picture. I am broke wif no mind. No past or present time. Only the movies of being someone else. Someone not fat, dark skin, short hair, someone not fucked. A pink virgin girl. A girl like Janet Jackson, a sexy girl don't no one get to fuck. A girl for value. A girl wif little titties whose self is luvlee just Luv-Vell-LEE!

I hate myself when I think Carl Kenwood Jones. Hate wif a capital letter. Counselor say, "Memories." How is something a memory if you never forgit? But I push it to the corner of my brain.

I exhausted, I mean wipe out! What kinda chile gotta think about a daddy like I do? But I'm not a chile. I'm a mother of a chile myself!

In school we had to memorize a poem like the rappers do. And say it in front the class. Everybody do real short poems except me and Jermaine. She do poem by lady name Pat Parker. I get up to do my poem, it's by Langston Hughes, I dedicate it to Abdul. Introduce myself to the class (even though everybody know me). I say my name is Precious Jones and this poem is for my baby son, Abdul Jamal Louis Jones. Then I let loose:


### Mother to Son

Well, son, I'll tell you:
Life for me ain't been no crystal stair.

It's had tacks in it,
And splinters,
And boards torn up,
And places with no carpet on the floor—
Bare.
But all the time
I'se been a-climbin' on,
And reachin' landin's,
And turnin' corners,
And sometimes goin' in the dark
Where there ain't been no light.
So boy, don't you turn back.
Don't you set down on the steps
'Cause you finds it's kinder hard.
Don't you fall now—
For I'se still goin', honey,
I'se still climbin',
And life for me ain't been no crystal stair.

And after I finish everyone goin', Yeah! Yeah! Shoutin', Go Precious! And clapping and clapping and clapping. I felt very good.

Ms Rain say write our fantasy of ourselves. How we would be if life was perfect. I tell you one thing right now, I would be light skinned, thereby treated right and loved by boyz. Light even more important than being skinny; you see them light-skinned girls that's big an' fat, they got boyfriends. Boyz overlook a lot to be wif a white girl or yellow girl, especially if it's a boy that's dark skin wif big lips or nose, he will go APE over yellow girl. So that's my first fantasy, is get light. Then I get hair. Swing job, you know like I do with my extensions, but this time it be my own hair, permanently.

Then, this part is hard to say, because so much of my heart is love for Abdul. But I be a girl or woman—yeah girl, 'cause I would still be a girl now if I hadn't had no kids. I would be a virgin like Michael Jackson, like Madonna. I would be a different Precious Jones. My bress not be big, my bra be little 'n pink like fashion girl. My body be like Whitney. I would be thighs not big etc etc. I would be tight pussy girl no stretch marks and torn pussy from babies's head bust me open. That HURT. Hours hours push push push! Then he out, beautiful. Jus' a beautiful baby. But I'm not. I'm eighteen years old. One time boy come to Advancement House to see girlfriend, he think I'm somebody's mother. That bother me.

So there if I have a fantasy it be how I look. Ms Rain say I am beautiful like I am. Where? How? To who? To not have no kids mean I woulda had a different life. Counselor ask me one time is it the kids or is it I get raped to have 'em. Bofe; 'cause even if I not raped, who want a baby at twelve! Thas how old I was when I had Little Mongo.

What is a normal life? A life where you not 'shamed of your mother. Where your friends come over after school and watch TV and do homework. Where your mother is normal looking and don't hit you over the head wif iron skillet. I would wish for in my fantasy a second chance. Since my first chance go to Mama and Daddy.

Ms Rain always saying write remember write remember. Counselor say talk about it, talk about it—the PAST. What about *NOW*! At least wif school I am gettin' ready for my future (which to me is right now).

I don't know why I don't like counselor but Ms Rain say TALK, it gonna make things better whether I like her or not. But you know she jus' another social worker scratching on a pad. I know she writing reports on me. Reports go in file. File say what I could get, where I could go—if I could get cut off, kicked out Advancement House. Make me feel like Mama.

Me and Ms Weiss in counsel room. She as' me what's my earliest memory of Mama.

Huh?

"What's your earliest memory of your mother?"

Last week it was Daddy Daddy. She on a "Mama" kick this week. I don't say nuffin'.

"Precious?"

I can't move, speak. It's like second grade again, paralyzed. Tired of this honky askin' me questions. And I do need someone to talk, but not this hoe. But the room here is nice, you know, big sunshine window, dark green leather furniture, pictures on wall. I'm on big green couch. She behind desk in swivel chair. On the side of her is file cabinets.

"Can I get you anything?"

"Soda." I don't say water. I could go get that myself. She know I ain' got no money. Only way I'm gonna get soda is if she buy me one. Machine down in laundry room. Advancement House rules—staff do not give clients money (let's face it some of these bitches who act so s'perior 'n shit usta be crack addicts).

"What kind?"

"Cherry Coke."

Soon as she close door behind her I'm up. Moving fast quiet. But inside slow torture walk like I'm walking through glue. Nervous, I can smell my sweat stinking. If she was to walk in on me now I turn around and slap her cracker ass down. Problem not crack but the CRACKER! Farrakhan say. Big beige file cabinet behind her desk. A–J one drawer, K–Z on next drawer. Jones, Jones (it's a very common name); no P Jones, oh thas right, they late! Got me under Claireece Jones. Yup, here it is, JONES, CLAIREECE P. 'n underneef my name, social security number, 015-11-9153. I *fly* back to big green chair, stuff file in my backpack. I'm wiping sweat off my forehead when Ms Weiss walk back in room.

"It is hot in here, isn't it?" she say.

"Yeah," I say. She hand me soda. I say thank you.

"Anything come up while I was gone?"

Shake my head.

"You know you can use your notebook in between sessions—"

"I do."

"I mean you can use it specifically for something like this, trying to recover your first memory of your mother."

I already know what I'm gonna recover, the smell of Mama's pussy in my face.

"What're you thinking?"

"Nothing."

"Well let me know what comes up for you during the week. Write it in your notebook OK?"

"OK."

"You know your mother's been calling here wanting to come visit."

"No, I didn't know that."

"Would you like to have her come into a counseling session with you?"

"I don't know, I never think about it before."

"Well one more thing to think about before I see you next week."

Get up, grab my backpack. "Bye," I say. Go upstairs to pay phones outside nursery, call Rita, she not home yet, she probably at one of her meetings. Call Jermaine, she home, don't tell her what I done did, jus' say it's real important can she git over here. She say yes.

When she git here I pull file out backpack, don't know why I didn't want to read it alone. Don't know if it's because I'm afraid of what it will say or if I'm afraid I won't be able to read it, maybe both. I start reading.

"I have just finished a session with Claireece Precious Jones. Precious, as she likes to be called, (I guess so bitch it's my name!) is an eighteen-year-old African

American female. According to her teachers at Each
One Teach One where she attends school she is a (I
don't know what that word is!) p-h-e-n-o-m-e-n-a-l
success." (Jermaine lean over my shoulder, say she not
sure about that one herself but judging from the con-
tents it must be good!) "Having made strides so tre—
men . . . tremendous! in the past year she was given the
mayor's award for outstanding achievement. She seems
to be actively en . . ." ("Engaged," Jermaine say) "in all
aspects of the learning process? However, (oh oh, when
white bitch start with *however*!) her TABE test scores
are disappointingly low." ("Not to Ms Rain! Not to Ms
Rain!" I say.) "She scored 2.8 on her last test." ("So
what! Ms Rain—" Jermaine interrupt, "Git a grip and
gon' read the report and don't get all emotional about
what this piece of shit white bitch got to say. Anyway, if
your shit wasn't dope you wouldn't be standin' up here
readin' what, what's her name?" "Ms Weiss." "What Ms
Weiss got to say.") "She will need at least an 8.0 before
she can enter G.E.D. class and begin work toward her
high school e-q . . . " ("Equivalency," Jermaine say. I
wanna say, I know, don't tell me the word 'less I ax! But
I never say anything like that to Jermaine.)

"Abdul is the client's (oh, now I'm *the client*) second
child; born in 1988, he's from all outwhere" (Jermaine
say, "That's 'outward' ") "OK, from all *outward* appear-
ances, a healthy and well adjusted toddler (he's a boy!).
Precious attends to his needs a-s-s-i-d-u-o-s-l-y (whatever!) and with great affection and ee-" ("Eagerly," Jer-

maine say) "seeks any and all information on child rear-
ing. (I guess so I'm his mother!) The client . . . " (I'm
the client again! I feel bullshit coming. I actually *feel*
sick. I hand the papers to Jermaine tell her, "Finish
reading.") "The client talks about her desire to get her
G.E.D. and go to college.

"The time and resources it would require for this
young woman to get a G.E.D. or into college would be
considerable. Although she is in school now, it is not a
job readiness program. Almost all instruction seems to
revolve around language a-c-" (Jermaine spelling now)
"q, a-kwi-si-tion acquisition!" ("What that?" I ask. "You
know, to get. Language acquisition, to get some language.") "The teacher, Ms Rain, places great emphasis
on writing and reading books. Little work is done with
computers or the variety of multiple choice pre-G.E.D.
and G.E.D. workbooks available at low cost to JPTA
programs.

"Precious is capable of going to work now. In January
of 1990 her son will be two years old. In keeping with the
new initiative on welfare reform I feel Precious would
benefit from any of the various workfare programs in
existence. Despite her obvious intellectual limitations
she is quite capable of working as a home attendant." ("A
home attendant? I don't wanna be no mutherfucking
home attendant! I wanna be—" "HUSH!" Jermaine say.)

"My rapport with Precious is minimal. Although I
am not sure with whom, she evidently has access to
counseling services provided by Each One Teach One.

She has a history of sexual abuse and is HIV positive."
("She say she not put that in my file! Bitch!" "If you told
it to her it's in there. That's that bitch's job, to get the
goods on you!" Jermaine say.) "The client seems to
view the social service system and its proponents as her
enemies, and yet while she mentions independent living, seems to envision social services, AFDC, as taking
care of her forever."

Jermaine hand me the file. "No way!" I scream. "I'm
getting my G.E.D., a job, and a place for me and Abdul,
then I go to college. I don't wanna 'home attend'
nobody."

"Be quiet!" Jermaine hiss. "And put this shit back
before you get in trouble!" I just sit there. She push the
file at me again. "Put this away. We'll talk about it with
Ms Rain in the morning."


"Let's put our chairs in a circle class," Ms Rain say, "and
do a little writing in our journals, then we'll talk. If you
want to focus on the topic introduced by Precious—"

"What topic?" Aisha, loud India girl from Guyana.

"Workfare and education."

"What about it?" Bunny, *real* skinny girl wif broke
teeth, say.

"Anything about it or nothing at all; if you want to
focus on the topic fine but you don't have to if you don't
want to. You have twenty minutes to write in your journal." She look at her watch, then say, "GO."

5/3/89

It's not like I in no big state of shock. I knew white bitch had something up her sleeve. Ms Weiss. Fuck her. I don't need her if all she see for me is wiping ol white people's ass. I ain been going threw all this learning to read and write so I be no mutherfucking home attendint. Rhonda usta hafta go all the way out to Brighton Beech wher she work for them mutherfuckers.

If I'm working twelve hours a day, sleeping in peoples houses like what Rhonda usta do, who will take care of Abdul? The ol white peoples had her there all day and night, "on call," they call it. But you only get pay for 8 hours (is the other 16 hours slavry?) so that's $8 \times \$3.35 = \$26.80$ dollars a day, but then you is not really getting that much cause you is working more than eight hours a day. You is working 24 hours a day and $26.80 divided by 24 is $1.12. Rhonda say ol bitch would ring a bell when she want Rhonda in the night. Home attendints usually work six days a week. I would only see Abdul on Sundays? When would I go to school? Why I gotta change white woman's diaper and then take money from that and go pay a baby sitter to change my baby's diaper? And what about school? How would I keep up with my reading and writing if I can't keep going to school?

I got to work it out before Abdul's birthday. Thas when the letters start coming. Letter say, you wish to keep receiving Aid to Families with Dependent Children report to XYZ place by such and such a date or your money will be cut. I mean I don't know exactly what it say but I got the drift, so many girls done told me what happen to them.

"OK," Ms Rain say. "Time is up for now, does anyone want to share?"

I'm only one raise my hand.

"OK Precious, go for it," she say.

"I don't really wanna read all I wrote, I jus' wanna kinda say what it is I'm writing about and how it came about. And how I'm really upset—"

"What *happened*?" Aisha say.

"Well to make a long story short the counselor at Advancement House pumping me about Mama and Daddy etc, etc, but it's really about workfare—"

"How you know?" Rhonda ax.

"'Cause I stole my file from Advancement House and read it. All this, 'What you wanna be?' and 'You can talk to me.' They ain' no mutherfucking therapists on our side they just flunkies for the 'fare."

Jermaine bust in. "If all they wanna do is place us in slave labor shits and we want to keep going to school, then that means they have a different agenda from us. I wanna work, but not for no mutherfucking welfare check in Central Park. And I be displacing brothers and sisters who really got jobs cleaning up 'cause I'm there working for free. And what kinda shit is it for someone like Precious to have to quit school before she get her G.E.D. to work at some live-in job for old crackers and shit. She'll never make a rise she get stuck in some shit like that!"

"Yeah," Ms Rain say, "but is stealing—"

"Ms Rain, I didn't steal that file I wouldn't know what my difficulties was!"

"You read the whole thing by yourself?" Ms Rain ask.

"Yeah, basically," I say, then, "Am I gonna hafta go be home attendant?"

"No!" Ms Rain say. "So stop worrying about it. We cross that bridge when we come to it. Trust me," she say, then, "No, trust *yourself.* But what I'm worried about right now is, if this Ms Weiss is someone they have you talking to to try to work out your history with and you can't trust her, you're not getting the help you need."

"Well, I just write in my notebook till I git wif some kinda therapist I can trust. Actually that help me more than talking to her. Plus I'm going to start going to meetings wif Rita for insect survivor—"

"*Incest,*" girl name Bunny say.

"Thas what I mean."

"Well, it ain't what you been saying."

"So, what's the big deal insect, incest?" I say.

"One's where your parents molest you, the other is like a roach or bugs," Bunny say.

I crack up laffing.

Ms Rain look at me funny and say, "Precious have you ever had your hearing tested?"

"No," I say. I have never really had nothing tested. Glasses is what I really want so my eyes not get so tired at night when I be reading. But you can't get all hung up on details when you trying to survive.

"OK, let's put our chairs back in rows and get to work on our business letters we started last week."

For the past week or so Jermaine been putting her story in the book. Title, just the title done upset the class, *Harlem Butch*. What kinda title is that! Jermaine done wrote it like a poem. She bes' writer. We can't wait to read it.

I write everyday now, sometimes for an hour. Ms Rain, she call and say I am staying late for after school activities and babysitter keep Abdul till 2 p.m. and the following week I get extra money in my voucher for lunch (not that I can eat lunch *today* wif money from next week, but you know still . . .). I think about my future a lot. I think a lot. All the time. Ms Rain say I am intellectually alive and curious. I am just trying to fig-ure out what is going on out here. How what happen to me could happen in modern days. I guess I am still try-ing to figure out just what *has* happen to me.

What has happen to me? I cannot just talk it to white social worker. She look at me like I am ugly freak did something to make my own life like it is. And she is try-ing to make me go to work wiping old white people's ass.

When I have a baby at twelve—

I don't want to cry. I tell myself I WILL NOT cry when I am writing, 'cause number one I stop writing and number two I just don't always want to be crying like white bitch on TV movies. Since I ain' no white bitch. I understand that now. I am not white bitch. I am not Janet Jackson or Madonna on the *inside*. I always thought I was someone different on the inside. That I was just fat and black and ugly to people on the OUT-SIDE. And if they could see *inside* me they would see something lovely and not keep laughing at me, throw-ing spitballs (shit one time nigger at school just spit on me when I was pregnant) and polly seed shells at me, that Mama and Daddy would recognize me as . . . as, I don't know, Precious! But I am not different on the inside. Inside I thought was so beautiful is a black girl too. But I am going to say what I was going to say. And then. I am going to put it all behind me and never say it again. I don't blame nobody. I just want to say when I was twelve, TWELVE, somebody hadda help me it not be like it is now. If—Ms Rain say "if" and "but" might be two of the most useless words in the language, at times that is, she say, 'cause if they was really useless they would disappear from use. Why no one put Carl in jail after I have baby by him when I am twelve? Is it my fault because I didn't talk to polices?

Tonight is the night Rita gonna take me down to Incest Survivor meeting. We going on bus. Harlem is small, but when you *in* it it look like the world. I have a subway map on my bedroom door, show all the places the subway go. Subway go to Queens, Brooklyn—I look at it sometimes and wonder where I be if I get on train and go to end of the line or get off at say, ummm, let's see, how about Lefferts Blvd in Queens or Middletown Road in the Bronx? What kinda town or part of New York it will be. Jermaine say be a white boy with a baseball bat when you get out of the subway. Rita say it's NOT true, or if it be true it's only part true.

So here I go! Precious going downtown. Precious what never go to summer camp; hear kids talk about going to camp where crackers is. Fresh Air funds and police league and shit. A land of tents and lakes. But maybe if I had gone to camp it be jus' like school in ol' days—no friends. Me 'n Rita get the 102 downtown. Rita done got her teef fixed. New guy she with got money. White guy. Got HIV too. He *loves* Rita. He was addict (I didn't know crackers was addicts). His parents stop giving him money when he was addict. But now he's sick they want to give him everything. Plus he got necktie job, briefcase, the whole bit. Rita got dream, he behind it. We all behind it. Rita want house in Harlem for HIV womens and their kids. I can get behind that. In my journal I write:

> bus wheel
> turn me
> through time
> past a Mama mama

first you see
the buildings like watching
a cartoon backwards
seem to be getting putted
back together
it's weird. (I am homer on a voyage
but from our red bricks in piles
of usta be buildings
and windows of black
broke glass eyes.
we come to buildings bad
but not *so* bad
street cleaner
then we come to a place
of
everything is fine
big glass windows
stores
white people
fur
blue jeans
its a different city
I'm in a different city
Who I be I grow up
here?
where a poodle dog
is not on tv
but walking down the street
on skinny white

bitch lease.
This whose ass
they want
me to wipe?
Push wheelchair for—
I kill 'em first.

TYGER TYGER
BURNING BRIGHT

That's what in Precious
Jones heart—a tyger.
bookstores
cafe
BLoomydales!
Bus keep on rolling


We git off at 14th Street. Rita say we can get cross-town bus or walk. I say walk; so we walk over to Seventh Avenue where Lesbian and Gay Center Building is. Rita not gay but this is where meeting is. We are going to Tuesday night Survivors of Incest Anonymous. I never been here before. Ms Rain, Rita, Rhonda, and Jermaine and house mom, all say GO. So I am good to go!

The center is big.

When I git in meeting I don't say nothing. It's people sitting in a circle. I'm spozed to talk. I will never talk here! To talk I have to tell how I feel in my body. The war. My body my head I can't say it right. How cum I'm so young and feel so old. So young like I don't know nuffin', so old like I know everything. A girl have her father's dick in her mouth know things the other girls don't know but it's not what you want to know.

It's all kinda girls here! They sitting in circle faces like clocks, no bombs. Bombs with hair and titties and dresses. After I sit here five minutes I know I am a bomb too. Only sitting here doing whatever they gonna do will keep me from blowing up. Thank you Rita for git me here on time.

"Hello." She look like a movie star! Slim, long hair, eyes like stars, red lips. "My name is Irene. I am an incest survivor."

My mouth fall open. Someone like that.

"It started when I was, oh, about four or five years old with him fondling me" (feeling her up). "By the time I was twelve he was having intercourse with me three or four times a week."

Everything is floating around me now. Like geeses from the lake. I see the wings beating beating hear geeses. It's more birds than geeses. Where so many birds come from. I see flying. Feel flying. *Am* flying. Far up, but my body down in circle. Precious is bird.

Someone is holding my hand. It's Rita. She is massage my hand. I come back from being a bird to hear beautiful girl crying. Smell Mama. Carl, the way his knees on either side of my neck.

Girl say, "Thank you for letting me share." She say, "This is a Tuesday night beginner's meeting. To share raise your hand." I raise my hand. My hand is going up through the smell of Mama, my hand is pushing Daddy's dick out my face.

"I was rape by my father. And beat." No one is talking except me. "Mama push my head down in her . . ." I can't talk no more. Beautiful girl whisper to me, "Are you through?" I say yes. She say, "Pick the next person." I look up from my shoes, Nikes; girls got they hand up. I pick girl in overalls with blue eyes. Grab Rita's hand, listen. Listen to girl rape by brother, listen to old woman rape by her father; don't remember till he die when she is 65 years old. Girls, old women, white women, lotta white women. Girl's younger sister murdered by the *cult*? Jewish girl, we had money on Long Island (like Westchester), my father was a prominent child psychiatrist. It started when I was about nine years old. Girls like Jermaine is, I am a proud lesbian. But it's the only thing I'm proud of; I was confine to a mental institution for fourteen years, diagnosed as a schizophrenia—

What am I hearing!

One hour and a half women talk. Can this be done happen to so many people? I know I am not lying! But is they? I thought cult was in movie. What kinda world this babies raped. A father break a girl's arm. Sweet talk you suck his dick. All kinda women here. Princess girls, some fat girls, old women, young women. One thing we got in common, no *the* thing, is we was rape.

Afterwards we go out for coffee. I have never been "out for coffee" before. Rita put her arm around my shoulder, I order hot chocolate 'cause that's what I like. Blond girl who is airline stewardess say, "Precious! That's a beautiful name!"

I'm alive inside. A bird is my heart. Mama and Daddy is not win. I'm winning. I'm drinking hot chocolate in the Village wif girls—all kind who love me. How that is so I don't know. How Mama and Daddy know me sixteen years and hate me, how a stranger meet me and love me. Must be what they already had in they pocket.

It's a black girl across the table from me with long pretty hair in dreadlocks like Ms Rain. But not wild like Ms Rain. I surprise myself. "How you get your hair like that?" I say.

"Oh," she say, "you like it? I do yours one day you want. That's what I do—fix people's hair and makeup." She give me a card!

Rita ask me do I want another hot chocolate. I do but don't want to be greedy. Even if boyfriend do give her money she got better things to spend it on then Precious Jones. She hug me and ask waitress, "Could I have another hot chocolate and cappuccino." I like how Rita is, she know the world, how to act and stuff. Sometimes I don't have a clue!

Well, today counseling session wif Mama. She call here, call here, *call* here, asking social worker to see me. I tell Ms Weiss no. Then Ms Weiss tell me I *should* see her. Why I should? I ask. For your own good, for yourself, to see what she has to say. Spozed to meet today 4 p.m.

Watch say one minute to four. Down one two three four five six seven eight steps, then a little landing then eight more steps. I walk through door, one minute past four. What she want now?

Mama sitting on big green couch. Ms Weiss looking at me waiting for me to sit down. I sit down. Ms Weiss say to Mama, "Well Mrs Johnston, may I call you Mary?"

"I don't care." Mama look down at her shoes which is big men's loafers. Room smell all funny. Mama stink. Got on big orange-color sleeveless dress, torn under the arms. Hair fucked up. Eyes look stupid wifout red evil light on to hit you.

I think Ms Weiss jus' freak mind. Lie to Mama, bull-corn me. Probably Mama think coming here talking to Ms Weiss in counselin' session gonna git me back, me 'n Abdul. So why do that? I don't git what Ms Weiss doin'. I need house for me 'n Abdul. Advancement House is for womens and girls with newborn and young babies. I gotta be out of this mutherfucker soon. I wanna finish at Each One Teach One 'n gone get my G.E.D. I want maybe git Lil Mongo out retard house where she lay on floor in pee clothes but Ms Weiss wanna know my earliest memory of Mama? I open my notebook and look in it.

whut is my erliest ~~memry~~ memory of my mother?
a room that's small fillt up wif my parents. it
smell. can of mackerel left open in kitchen on hot

day that's what make me remember. that smell. he
put his ball in my face. years like wash machine
aroun and around. mama jaw open like evil wolf.
the smell deeper than toilet. her fingers pick
apart my pussy. night. poisoned rat. don't have
dreams.

I close my book.

"Well Mary, you want to begin by talking a little bit
about the abuse?" Ms Weiss say to Mama.

"What 'buse?"

"Well according to Precious' files she has had two
children by your boyfriend, the late Carl Kenwood Jones,
who is also *her father*? You've been calling here saying you
want to be reunited with your daughter and grandson,
that you want them to come home. Well I think you'd
better explain just what happened in that home."

Oh Mama, please don't go for this!

"Well, I, Precious, b'long at home."

Mama please be quiet.

"When did the abuse happen, how often, where?
When were you first aware of what was going on Ms
Johnston?"

"I guess, he come over you know. I wake up at night,
morning he not wif me, I know he in there wif her.
When it first start? I don' know. I'm a good mother. She
had everything. I done tole her that. Pink 'n white baby

carriage, little pink bootie socks, dresses; everything I put on her pink. Precious, she, so smiling and healthy. A day don't go by I don't take her out wheeling in the air. Even when it's cold I take her out, to church, to somewhere, me 'n Carl—my husband, I call him—loves Precious. I loves him. I dream of day we gonna you know, git married, git house wif grass, color TVs in all the rooms. Precious she born about the same time as Miz West son that got kilt. You remember him don't you Precious?"

What is she talkin' about!

"He born summertime 'bout same time as you."

"I born November," I say. Least that what I always thought.

"Yeah yeah thas right. My little Scorpio chile! Scorpio's crafty. I ain' sayin' they lie, jus' you cain't always trust 'em. But anyway Precious 'bout the same age as Gary, Miz West son got kilt, give or take a few months! But ooh wheee! Precious fast! She walkin' talkin'— everything 'fore Miz West son. Her teef, everything. Teef growing like Bugs Bunny or something! She can do little dance steps and he hardly walking, you put on Kool and the Gang, remember Precious, you remember? I put on Kool and the Gang and you disco to that? She had a happy childhood all 'n all, Carl jus' a high-natured man . . ."

I don't believe Mama! Why don't she jus' shut up with this diarrhea shit!

"When? I don't know when it start. When I remember it? She still little. Yeah, around three maybe. I give her a bottle. I still got milk in my bresses but not for her but from Carl sucking. I give him tittie, Precious bottle. Hygiene, you know?"

"Huh?" Ms Weiss go.

"Huh?" go Mama back.

"You mentioned something about hygiene in connection with . . . with . . . " Ms Weiss can't finish.

"I bottle her, tittie him. Bottle more better for kidz. Sanitary. But I never git dried up 'cause Carl always on me. It's like that you know. Chile, man—a woman got bofe. What you gonna do? So we in bed. I put her on one side of me on pillow, Carl on other side me."

Ms Weiss look like she done stopped breathing.

"Carl got my tittie in his mouf. Nuffin' wrong wif that, it's natural. But I think thas the day IT start. I don't never remember nothing before that. I hot. He sucking my tittie. My eyes closed. I know he getting hard I can see wifout my eyes, I love him so much."

Umm hmm, I was raised by a psycho maniac fool.

"He climb on me, you know. You unnerstand?"

No, tell us some more stupid bitch.

"So he on me. Then he reach over to Precious! Start wif his finger between her legs. I say Carl what you doing! He say shut your big ass up! This is good for her. Then he git off me, take off her Pampers and try to stick his thing in Precious. You know what trip me out is it almost can go in Precious! I think she some kinda freak baby then. I say stop Carl stop! I want him on *me*! I never wanted him to hurt her. I didn't want him doing *anything* to her. I wanted my man for myself. Sex me up, not my chile. So you cain't blame all that shit happen to Precious on *me*. I love Carl, I love him. He her daddy, but he was my man!"

Ms Weiss look at me now. "Precious, you've been writing in your journal about this."

"This and other stuff."

"She write poems too, lady at Each One Teach One say." This from Mama. Mama one hundred, not ninety nine, percent crazy.

"Would you like to share some of that in this session?" Ms Weiss ask.

"No."

"Why not?"

"Ms Rain say journal completely confidential. Share if you want. If you don't want to, don't. I don't want to."


I'm gone. It's 4:45 p.m. Up! One, two, three, four, five, six, seven, eight steps. I hate Mama, she ain' shit. I feel like nothing around her, like *minus* nothing. I gotta get outta here.

I go down to kitchen where house mother is. "Miz Mom!"

"Stop screaming!" she say. "What's wrong with you?"

"You could get Abdul from nursery, feed him, and

keep a eye on him till I get back so I could go to Body Positive meeting?"

"Tonight's not your night—"

"Pleeezzze I gotta get outta here!"

"What happened with your mama?"

" 'You cain't blame all what happened to Precious on *me*. I wanted *my man* for *myself!*' " I imitate Mama.

"I wanted my man for myself! Now ain' that one to go down in the history books. Yeah, I'll keep that little ol' bad boy! You got a lot of time before six-thirty, why don't you git you some dinner before you run out of here?"

"I was gonna take my journal book and write on the bus, 'steadda taking the train."

She go in her pocket get out that ol' blue change purse, so ol' it look like somebody blue grandmother and hand me three dollars. Something tear inside me. I wanna cry but I can't. It's like something inside me keeps ripping but I can't cry. I think how *alive* I am, every part of me that is cells, proteens, nutrons, hairs, pussy, eyeballs, nervus sistem, brain. I got poems, a son, friends. I want to live so bad. Mama remind me I might not. I got this virus in my body like cloud over sun. Don't know when, don't know how, maybe hold it back a long long time, but one day it's gonna rain.

I start to cry but it's 'cuz I'm mad. Miz Mom wipe my face give me two more dollars!

"Umm, I should cry more often!"

"Ain' you about a mess! Git outta here!"

I git my jacket 'n my shades. Everybody in this house

go to meetings, in "recovery." What I'm in recovery for? I ain' no crack addict. I git so mad sometimes. Mama jus' pour my life down the drain like it's nothing. I got all this shit to deal wif.

"Don't forget your notebook," Miz Mom.

Everybody know I write poems. People respect me. I get outside. It's raining. Good.


The meeting is good, it's for HIV positive girls 16–21. Ms Rain say people who help you most (*sometimes*) is ones in the same boat. I started putting my story in the big book at school. I want to get it done before I graduate out to G.E.D.

Last week we went to the museum. A whole whale is hanging from the ceiling. Bigger than big! OK, have you ever seen a Volkswagen car that's like a bug? Um huh, you know what I'm talking about. That's how big the heart of a blue whale is. I know it's not possible, but if that heart was in me could I love more? Ms Rain, Rita, Abdul?

I would like to.

Abdul get tested. He is not HIV positive. Something like that make me feel what Rhonda, what Farrakhan, say—there is a god. But me when I think of it I'm more inclined to go wid Shug in *The Color Purple*. God ain' white, he ain' no Jew or Muslim, maybe he ain' even black, maybe he ain' even a "he." Even now I go downtown and seen the rich shit they got, I see what we got too. I see those men in vacant lot share one hot dog and they homeless, that's good as Jesus with his fish. I remember when I had my daughter, nurse nice to me—all that is god. Shug in *Color Purple* say it's the "wonder" of purple flowers. I feel that, even though I never seen or had no flowers like what she talk about.

I'm not happy to be HIV positive. I don't understand why some kids git a good school and mother and father and some don't. But Rita say forgit the WHY ME shit and git on to what's next.

I don't know what's next. I took the TABE test again, this time it's 7.8. Ms Rain say quantum leap! Like I was one place and instead of step up, it's a leap! What does that score actually mean? I read according to the test around 7th or 8th grade level now. Before on test I score 2.0 then 2.8. The 2.0 days was really low days because I could not read at all (test just give you 2.0 even if you don't fill in nothing). I got to get up to the level of high school kids, then college kids. I know I can do this. Ms Rain tell me don't worry it's gonna work out. I still got time.

It's Sunday, no school, meetings. I'm in dayroom at Advancement House, sitting on a big leather stool holdin' Abdul. The sun is coming through the window splashing down on him, on the pages of his book. It's called *The Black BC's*. I love to hold him on my lap, open up the world to him. When the sun shine on him like this, he is an angel child. Brown sunshine. And my heart fill. Hurt. One year? Five? Ten years? Maybe more if I take care of myself. Maybe a cure. Who knows, who is working on shit like that? Look his nose is so shiny, his eyes shiny. He my shiny brown boy. In his beauty I see my own. He pulling on my earring, want me to stop daydreaming and read him a story before nap time. I do.

<u>LIFE STORIES</u>

Our Class Book


Reading 1   MWF 9-12 a.m.

Higher Education Alternative /
Each One Teach One

Blue Rain, Instructor

*everi mornin*
by Precious j.

Everi mornin
i write
a poem
before I go to
school
marY Had a little lamb
but I got a kid
an HIV
that folow me
to school
one day.

*mornin*
by Precious Jones


Mornin is a rooteen
up at 6 a.m.
wash teef, dress
    wash Abdul teef, face, booty
    dress him
Breakfast for kids
    we go to kitchen
    fix him something
    good from what's there
    what's there for baby
    is good
oatmeal
cream wheat
rice cream
appul sauc
    or egg toast
    bacon    I don't let Abdul eat bacon
Put Abdul wif a kiss
    in nother woman arms

```
rootine b
          r
           e
            a k
i run get dress
      fix tea (don't like coffee)
      grab books
                walk
      mornin wet the streets
      amung the vakent trees
           is secrit plots
           of green diamonds
           call grass.
```

*MY LIFE*
by Rita Romero


Our house, which was an apartment, was full of beautiful stuff—velvet couch, lace curtain, virgin statues, candles, and chandeliers. My mother was like a medium. Not santeria—throw shells, yellow flowers for Oshun and all that but more the gypsy trip—cards and crystal ball. Always people in and out our house; nice people, give me a caramel or sourball, pat on the head. My mother was dark, moreno? Like we got 1 million words for color, Puerto Ricans. But to me, everyone, she was beautiful. She look like, you ever seen that movie star from way back, Dorothy Dandridge—that's what Momi look like, only Momi's hair is like a black river, thick long down her back. Eyes, I always think Momi's eyes is olives. Black things that could see but so rich you could eat. Maybe, I giggle, if you could eat Momi's eyes you could see in the crystal ball too.

My father honestly I don't remember him so much even though I know he was there everyday. I know he is white because he tells me this, tells me I am white. I wanna be what Momi is, not what he is. Momi says he is just another brainwashed spic. He had a shop on Tremont Ave where he work on wreck cars. From Momi is beans and rice, roast pork, flan, the pink and yellow lace dresses I wear to Mass. From him is be quiet be quiet go help your mother clean this place up it's a mess it's a mess speak English speak English SPEAK ENGLISH. It's because of him I don't speak Spanish. He tell Momi talk English talk English make the kids speak English. You want 'em to grow up like you puta can't get a job. Puta, whore bitch I know what you're doing with these guys while I'm out working my ass off. I ever catch I kill you whore, hear me I kill you. Then he grab me, hold out my arm next to his, see SEE. Look he says you are WHITE. You are not no nigger morena puta WHORE. He's crazy he don't make sense. Momi is not that. He scream at

Momi, "My kids are WHITE!" Momi just look scared.

I'm six years old. The walls of the room are maroon. The velvet couch with the white lace doilies is the same color as the wall. It is so pretty. It's my favorite. In the middle is the dark wood table with the crystal ball. Lace curtains is on the window. The shades is drawn. What's inside is prettier, outside is just a brick wall. The table has a glass top on it. The edges of the glass where it's cut is green colored, I like that. The crystal ball is big. Momi is at the table, her hair is black down her back, her lips like red movie star lips, eyes black like oil, looking at me. She hands me a sourball, it's my favorite; it's melting in my mouth. By the time it melts I know she be going shoo shoo Negra, I got someone coming. Meaning one of the worry face clients talking in Spanish about somebody dead, in jail or in the arms of another, would be there.

But the taste of the sour ball stays on my tongue forever. It's Papi walk through the door. He don't say Mamita, he say Bitch! You think I'm crazy. I KNOW que tu puede. I KNOW PUTA! And he pull gun from his pants, shoot Momi— bang bang bang. Her brains fly out her head her mouth open blood blood blood everywhere, it look like one olive is hanging out her head like a man off a cliff. She never speak nothing, fall out chair, go gurgle sound, more blood fall out her mouth. Her dress, hair, the carpet is red. Papi standing there, start crying.

If I close my eyes I could see Puerto Rico—someplace water is blue jewels, palm trees, mangoes, music like Willie Colon all the time. But I never been there. Would it be different if I had been born there steadda here? He kill her there steadda here? What's the difference? Go back? To where you never been? I'm better off here with the AIDS thing and stuff. The health care ain't shit here for addicts but it's better than P.R. my brother say. He went to P.R. die. I got friends here and stuff.

Ms Rain, senora La Lluvia, ask me to write more, write about my life now. Just talk some more in the tape recorder and she transcribe it. What life? Foster care, rape, drugs, prostitution, HIV, jail, rehab. Everybody like to hear that story. Tell us more tell us more more MORE about being a dope addict and a whore! Puta tecata puta tecata. But I tell you what *I* want, it's *my* book—we had a nice place, velvet things, lace curtains, the crystal ball. I ask her once my hand in the black river of her hair, my eyes looking up at hers, her caramel color skin, red movie lips, the perfume from her like a pink and purple dream—show me Momi how to see. Show me what's inside the crystal ball. She look at long time then say, Ahh Negrita, you don't want to know.

### *MY YOUNGER YEARS*
### by Rhonda Patrice Johnson

My younger years was actually spend in Jamaica which is where my family is from. It was me my brother and my mother and father who we call Ma and Pop. Things was good there until Pop die then we didn't have money so we move to the U.S. For me that is when the problem start. What the problem is is hard to say but it was with my brother.

My mother git a restaurant on 7th Ave. between 132nd and 133rd selling West Indian take out. I work in the restaurant from git up in the morning to go to bed at night. I don't go to school even. I could read and write some but when we got here I was twelve already and hadn't been going to school for a long time in Jamaica. So my mother say, you almost grown so what's the use. But Kimberton, he's my brother go to school. A lot go for Kimberton—clothes, bicycle, computer toy. He is one year younger than me. I wash down the kitchen, scrub pots, pans, grill, all that! Go to the big market with Ma at Hunt's Point. Go to La Marqueta on Lexington with Ma. I make peas and rice, roti, cod fish cakes, goat curry, all that! The people that want eat in we got two little tables in the front near the window. I serve people.

I fourteen when Kimberton start leaning on me. I don't know how else to tell it.

"Ma, Kimberton leaning on me."

"What you telling?"

"He bothering me."

"Leave his computer stuff alone and he will leave your dolls alone."

That's what he used to do in Jamaica, break my dolly's head or arm off. I mean something different now. He is the same size as me. I try to fight him. We sleep in same room. He wait until I am sleep. I awake Kimberton standing over me on top the bed naked as the day he born. Thing like a donkey's. I don't want it. My skin get bad. I don't know if it's from that. I get a lot of pounds on me. I'm always a quiet girl, I don't say NOTHING now unless some one speak me.

I tell her again when I am 16. Kimberton is fifteen but he skipped a grade in elementary school so he is in his second year of high school. Going to be a doctor. "You going to be a doctor!" my mother tell him, "What you think I'm working for, for you to be a god damn taxi driver!" the question I ask myself is, what am I working for.

"Ma."

"What!"

"Kimberton is . . . is molesting with me at night." I don't know how to say it. I can't say rape, that's not what brothers do to sisters.

"Molesting with you? What kinda talk is that?"

"You know—"

"No, I don't know! Miss Fresh."

"He come over my side of the room at night and intercourse me."

She get quiet quiet. I smell the curry goat stewing, peas 'n rice. I can

see through the glass door of refrigerator bottles of ginger beer, 7UP, Cokes
and maubey lined.

"Tell me what you talking about."

I tell her.

She say get out my house now. I say
but Ma! Leave now she start screaming
'bout what I done to her son. Filthy
haint, night devil walker she call me.
I am shocked. I think I am still in that
shock sometimes.


But it's like that sometime you know.
I done found out over the years you just
can't guess how people is gonna react.
You think common sense would make her
come out on my side. You know, mother
daughter, but it didn't happen that
way. She was screaming 'bout how I was
the oldest coulda shoulda stopped him.
what I believe is she think Kimberton
gonna be big doctor one day and retire
her from working twenty-four seven. An'
if someone got to go it not gonna be
him.

part two

*MY GROWN UP YEARS*

I'm twenty-four years old it's been eight years since I "left" (I put it like that cause you know how I left) my mother's house. Kimberton, he is dentist. Was a dentist, maybe he is, maybe he beat the case—he get charged by young girl's parents of trying to stick his finger (and who knows what else) up her pussy while he spozed to be fixing teeth! Far out huh? Ma tell me this. I don't go visit but I see her out on street when she doing her shopping. We talk like I'm her daughter that got married and move out or go away to nurse school or some such. I don't know, I just go along with the program. Ma say it's all lies, girl's parents just trying to extort him. But what I think is he pull his shit on the wrong one. You can't get away with everything all the time with everybody.

The first couple of years on the street was the worst. From working

under Ma, even though I do everything,
I really did not know how to get a job,
talk to social service—what's that! So
I was just out there! I would go with
men to bars, drink, go home with them,
hope I get to stay the night—that they
don't tell me go after they come. After
I do this with, oh, is it five or fifty
or a hundred guys, I start dissolve. I
don't know how else to explain it. I'm
strong woman, if you was looking at me
you could see this. Redbone, what Amer-
icans say, some color to her, Jamaicans
would say. Five foot eight inches,
heavy set, or fat some people would say.
Kimberton (who is dark) say I look like
a mutant, what ever that is. But after
the I don't know how many mens I start
to break into little pieces and the men
look funny, like worms is growing out of
their skins, worms that turn to little
penises, till I am sick with the walking dicks of Harlem. Everywhere is a
hand rubbing, a dick going psst psst
come here come here.

I can't stay in shelters. I just
can't, they is crazy people houses. So

I just wander the street, get little money here and there. I meet this one guy, give me enough to get a room at the Y for one week, tell me to go down to welfare. I check that out. They are so nasty to me, send me so many different places to get so many different papers, things I don't have no way of getting! I don't have no birth certificate unless my mother got it but I know where I was born—Kingston, Jamaica. September 22, 1963. I say fuck the whole welfare thing. It's crazy. I walk out office but not before I break one white woman's nose. She send me to get a social security card. I tell her the number but she say got to have the card, go get a duplicate at downtown office. By the time I get back from downtown, where they tell me was an office I could go to on 125th Street, she got coat on talking 'bout she through for the day, going home. You know just as breezy as she can be! Come back tomorrow and she help me right off. What she saying, and she know it, spend another night in nowhere sleeping next to death. Git on that park bench, subway, rooftop—freeze, get stabbed, raped; I'm going home. I haul off and hit that bitch so hard whole room could hear her nose go CRUNCH.

At the Y this woman from Trinidad tell me about ol' white bitch in Brighton Beach she taking care of but she gonna hafta quit cause she got something better on Upper West Side wheeling some doctor's children to the park. Say she recommend me, don't need no social security card and all that.

So I work for ol' white woman with degenerative disease and mind to equal. HATE black people, always a "you people this" and "you people that." Call me to her daughter Swortkraus! "Swortkraus is a little slow today," what kinda goddam shit is that. But you know she ol' and helpless I forgive a lot. I think I could put a pillow over her face and no one know, no one care. But I would know, plus I be out of a job. I leave when she throw, try to, throw bed pan at me (end up spilling it on her self) cause she grandson, who she putting through NYU medical school did not come to see her when he say he would. She good and crazy.

I go back to welfare, this time I say to myself, some money or jail. All the Porta Ricans and American niggers can get something—white people is getting it too. Why can't I?

The security guards get me while my thumbs is closing down on this white devil's throat. Tell me cool down mama! I'm not your mama! Everything is red, I go end this cracker's days! They pull me off, take four of 'em. I don't go to jail though. They get me job! One of the black guys, not even a desk to himself, hand me a three by five card with a name and address on it, tell me, go there. I get position looking after ol' white man, tubes all in him. He not so bad, but he nasty. Want me to wash his penis and carry on. On all the walls, I mean on every wall, is a picture, I mean a big picture of Michael Jordan. OK, 16 walls, you got it, 16 pictures of Michael Jordan.

But he pay me. I get room with bathroom, things looking up for awhile, you know. Then the ol' mutherfucker die. After a while it's pretty hard again. I get three day notice to pay or quit my room. What I'm gonna do? I'm a person don't just like to sit there. Just sit there I be throw out for sure. I get couple of big big garbage bags and start going from trash can to trash can collecting aluminum cans. To fill the bags take awhile cause is some competition out on the Harlem streets for these bottles and cans. But I am strong and desperate. I'm looking like a beetle bug or something, hunched over with two huge black garbage bags on my back. I'm on Adam Clayton Powell Blvd which I usually avoided cause it's where Ma's restaurant, ROTI 'N MORE Take Out or Eat In, is. But today I don't care, I don't wanna be homeless again. It happen again I might not get up from it. I gotta do something.

So I'm on the Avenue (which is also the Boulevard) near 134th Street moving, trash can by trash can, toward 133rd. I pass ROTI 'N MORE. I look up and see a FOR RENT sign in the window, and next to sign is Kimberton. Our eyes meet. His is shock, mine is like a kiss, my brother! Always my first thought of him is before he rape me then the memory roll in like fog. I see Kimberton's mouth fall open at the horror of me bent over, hands gripped around the black bags. I remember my hands grating coconut, washing rice, stirring peas, scrubbing pots in cold greasy water, pulling the catheter out the old man's penis, scraping shit from old Mrs Feld's age spot ass. I look back at him. I am not ashamed. I could be dead all these years. Rage hot fill me. Kimberton's eyes glowing like radioactive in my mind, his fly eyes, his hands pushing me down on the bed, years. Years. Kimberton comes to the door. He has on some clothes that cost a lot and should look great but he just look foreign and skinny and dark. He don't look like American man like he want to. I stare. This a man fuck his sister and say so what. This a man go to dental school, graduate high school at sixteen. A credit to his family and race, Ma say. But I'm his family and race ain't I?

"What do you want?" he say.

I don't speak.

"Ma already buried. No one can find you to tell you."

Ma dead? A fog like a coming down on me. Kimberton step toward me, pull one hundred dollar bill from his wallet. To take it I would have to put the bags down. I look down at Kimberton's orange colored leather shoes, stupid pointed toes, and up to his head which is begin- ning to bald.

I figure I better get moving 'fore the fog is too thick to see my way out. Kimberton is walking behind me now say- ing stupid things. "We wondered about you." It's like some kinda dribble, his voice, that fall on top the fog. "You wanted it as much as I did!" he say. How could he say that. I keep walking, such a long way I have to go.

It's a guy at the soup kitchen, Asian guy, advocate from Young and Homeless, find out I got a work history get me job

cleaning office building over in East
Harlem. I get me a room over on Convent
Avenue from old light-skinned dude got
one of those big old prewar apartments,
renting out rooms. Tell me when his
mother had the place she rent room to
Marcus Garvey. My question is, did Marcus Garvey get heat? It's at rooming
place I meet Rita Romero, who is in
class, who tell me about school which is
how I get in this book.

the end, no the BEGINNING

## *HARLEM BUTCH*
### by Jermaine Hicks

Why you wanna be a man?
Why you wanna be a man
man
man
why you wanna be
a man?
why you wanna be
a man
man
man?

Look it never occurred to me to dress
like man! For Chrissake, what the fuck
is that? I was dressing like myself.
Myself.
I'm 7:
"Hurry up! Get dressed or you'll be
late for school!" my mother is shouting. The whole block can hear her for
sure. She has a mouth like an express
train. She has to be out the door by
eight to make sure she's not late for

the white woman she works for. My father is already gone by 6 a.m. Every morning. I look down from the top of the bunk beds to my brother's empty unmade bed. The sheet is a gray tangle twisting out underneath dingy blue poly blankets. His brown corduroy pants are red flags signalling something in my 7 year old soul. I jump out the top bunk, pick up the pants and put them on. That was seventeen years ago. They were not my pants but I felt they should be. I, how to describe a feeling so deep it's like a river? How can a river be wrong?

"Take off those pants!"
"No!"
"Those are your brother's pants."
"Git me some."
"They're not lady like."
"So what!"
"It's wrong!"
"Why?"
How can a river be wrong
a river that engorges my clitoris
and fills me?

. . .

Ms Rain, rivers, what makes rivers
run?
"Huh?"
A river, what makes it go, run?
"Well, I don't really know. I never
studied rivers in college. I mean, I
imagine some type of gravity, the
riverbed's resistance to absorption;
you know rainfall,
water running so down hill—"
A river ever run wrong?
"What?"
Run wrong, a river ever run wrong?
"Well, they overflow—flood—"
(she flailed .
Yes, that was the word, flailed,
flailed helplessly Ms. Rain did.
"In 1811, the Mississippi flowed
backwards due to an earthquake."
If I didn't have a record I'd join
the Navy,
Be ON water, IN water all the time!
(I could have passed my G.E.D. test
months, no a year ago. Ms Rain is
upset I won't take it. Taking it

will mean I will have to leave the
class.)
I'm still 7:
a boy holds me down
under the stairwell
that smells like urine
(pee I woulda said at seven)
tries to push his dick
into me.
I am 8:
when I put my tongue
in Mary-Mae's mouth
for the first time
(under the same steps)
9:
my fingers
10:
my tongue but this time
I put in her
where he tried to put
it in me
13:
I am pressed close to her
against the wall
in her room
we will fall on the
still pink in some places

chenille bedspread
My fingers A trains howling thru her
dark tunnel
We will—
DADDY! DADDY!
Come LOOK what Mary-Mae and Jermaine
is doing!
BULLDAGGERBULLDAGGERBULLDYKE
DYKEBULLDYKEBULLDYKEDYKEDYKE
the voices become like the programmed messages in the subway time
unpredictable loud irritating
expected
but it is Mary-Mae's father who
catches me one night to show me
what a MAN is, what a woman is
when I get up from my new knowledge
one of my front teeth is gone
The doctor will tell my mother
damage is done
I won't tell her by who


I never told that part of my story
before because I hate to see their
square eyes light up with, "Oh that's
why! I understand now! I see—"

No! You don't see! Before I was snatched out the air like a butterfly, wings torn off me. BEFORE any all that I had slid my fingers up the sweet stink of another child and knelt down to lick her thighs. Men did not make me this way. Nothing happened to make me this way. I was born butch!

I was 14:

my mother is a religious movement. I don't know how else to describe it, a walking church. A wake up, go to sleep, jack off, shouting ass Christian. It make me sick. JESUS this, JESUS that, fuck that shit.


We are nuclear but poor
four of us
mother father sister brother sitting around the white formica covered table, little flecks of gold embedded like sunshine in the white plastic. We are eating breakfast, which is sardines out a can emptied onto our plates and some cold biscuits left over from last night. He went to take a sip of coffee and she

said, "According to Luke Chapter 9, verse 16, Jezus took the five loaves and the two fishes and looking up at heaven—" And his arm flew out like a jack-in-the-box and snatched the Bible from her and threw it in her face HARD. Hitting her in the eye. A blood red spot grew and spread across her eye for seven days. By the time she went to Emergency she was another colored woman shoulda come in sooner story there's not really much we can do for you now except call in the medical students from NYU to stare at how stupid you people are and you can learn to see almost as well with one eye as you can with two.

So my mother—one eye, no man, two children and the Bible.

What hurt more than the dark hole of Daddy's leaving, than Mary-Mae's father raping me, more than seeing the spot grow in Mama's eye like a radioactive tomato, was seeing her afterward on the D train, holding her Bible over her head screeching, "HELL! You are going to hell! Unless you accept the word of God's only son JEEZUSS!! JEEEEEZZUUSSS!!! The train hurtling through the dark tunnel, the laughing pitying and annoyed eyes of the riders and my mother, blind eye, a snot colored marble in her chocolate face screaming, "JEZUS! JJEEEEEE-ZZZZUUUUUUSSSS!!!!!"

I'm 17:

when she walks in on me and Mary-Mae fucking. Can't she see we're in love?

No, she can't.

She starts to foam at the mouth screaming curses in the name of God. FILTHYSICKHELPMEJEZUSIDIDNTRAISEYOU-THISWAYFILTHYFILTHY The words float over our naked bodies like clouds of poison gas. They drop on us soiling Mary-Mae's long copper legs, smooth child free body. The smell of us sweet, stinky, swollen with sex contracts and dies in the air.

I love Mary-Mae.

I pull my underpants, jeans, shirt, shoes on, all in one seemingly impossible move. Mary-Mae is in a daze. The poison gas shaming her causing her to stumble. We fall out the room together and then the front door of the apartment. Mary-Mae turns down the hall to her father's apartment. I keep going until I hit the street. I never see Mary-Mae again.

I'm seventeen and parent free. An emancipated minor. I mean my father was not hard to find. In a tiny studio in Queens, where, "I'm welcome to stay as long as I want." But at night when he flops down on the convertible sofa, the kind you see advertised on the subway for five hundred dollars, I am left on a thin mat near the door listening to him masturbate. Does he think I'm asleep? In the morning over a breakfast of boiled eggs and salmon cakes that reminds me of sardines, he asks me if the floor isn't hard. The sardines remind me how swift and long his arms are. The sun coming through his window is a blood red spot that covers the sky.

So I step out on the street that morning, on my own, like Huck Finn or some shit, it's been like that ever since—Harlem, The Village, The Bronx, Queens—I know my way around. I bartend, drive cab, do maintenance. I was super over on 126th and Madison for three years. But I want more than pushing a mutherfuck-ing broom, or slooshing fire juice to other broom pushers. So I came back to school. I knew from day one I should be in G.E.D. class but I know I never woulda wrote this story with those dickheads in there. I never would have stayed.

My face? My eye, ear? Ms Rain say you might want to write about that? Write about six grown men,

I'm 19: by then. What can I say except I fought back. And when it's six men that means you put your fist up and try to hit at least one of 'em 'fore they kill you. I'm with Rita, on that some things don't need to be written about. For example, how it sounds when a fist with two hundred pounds behind it con-nects solidly with your eye. Or the way concrete does not yield to lip cheek nostril when they meet. And a razor, the closest thing it feels like is extreme cold. Cold so cold it's hot, a laser separating.

I woke up in Harlem Hospital. Like Mama one eye messed up ear too. But the Bible did not save me. I saved myself. Am still saving myself. That was the second time men took me to school. Only time I don't have a gun on me now is when I go to sleep, even then, Mary-Mae, as I call my rod, is not far away.

It's not over yet!

*Jermaine*

*untitled*
by Precious Jones


Rain, wheels, bus
car,
only in dreams
I have car
me n Abdul riding like
in the movies
sun a yellow red ball
rising over hills
where indeins usta live
beaches, Islands
where Jamaica-talks live
Bob Marley
song
first I don't unnerstan it
but now I do
CONCREET JUNGLE
it's a prison days
we live in
at least me
I'm not really free
baby, Mama, HIV
where I wanna be where i wanna be?
not where I AM

on the 102
down lex avenue
I do have
lungs take in air
I can see
I can read
nobody can see now
but I might be a poet, rapper, I got
  water colors
my child is smart
my CHILDREN
is alive
some girls in
forin countries
babies dead.
Look up sometimes
and the birds
is like dancers
or
like programmed
by computer
how they fly
tear up
your heart
bus moving
PLAY THE HAND YOU GOT
housemother say.

HOLD FAST TO DREAMS
Langston say.
GET UP OFF YOUR KNEES
Farrakhan say.
CHANGE
Alice Walker
say.
Rain fall down
wheels turn round
DON'T ALWAYS RHYME
Ms Rain say
walk on
go into the poem
the HEART of it
beating
like
a clock
a virus
tick
tock.

1991

A NOTE ON THE TYPE

This book was set in Janson, a typeface long thought to have been made by the Dutchman Anton Janson, who was a practicing typefounder in Leipzig during the years 1668–1687. However, it has been conclusively demonstrated that these types are actually the work of Nicholas Kis (1650–1702), a Hungarian, who most probably learned his trade from the master Dutch typefounder Dirk Voskens. The type is an excellent example of the influential and sturdy Dutch types that prevailed in England up to the time William Caslon (1692–1766) developed his own incomparable designs from them.

Composed by North Market Street Graphics,
Lancaster, Pennsylvania
Printed and bound by Berryville Graphics,
Berryville, Virginia
Designed by Virginia Tan